"W _____ **e**
exactly _____ **see and**
_____ **ve. Wha** _____ **is** ?
may __ **you** _____ **about what**
you feel—even about who you are.
Don't know why. Not going to guess."

He grabbed her arm and pulled her back to him. "But I have a confession of my own to make. I'm attracted to you. And when you talked about men looking at you…I looked."

She looked up into his eyes. Swallowed hard. "But we can control the urges, Reid."

"Because we want to, or because we have to?"

Nothing in her wanted to, because she liked the way he held on to her—his grip not rough, yet not gentle. And she liked his dominance. It was firm, but not unrelenting. _E_

"Because it's the only practical thing to do."

"Depends on your definition of practical," he said, pulling her up against his chest.

Keera looked up, put her hands on the sides of his face to hold him where she wanted him—which was no place but here, in this moment, this _only_ moment. Then she wound her fingers up through his hair, tugged it slightly, and smiled when he started to breathe faster. Breaths to match hers. The edges of their bodies were melting into each other.

W

Dear Reader

Years ago, my husband and I met a wonderful little boy named Ryan. Ryan was an amazing kid—smart, full of life, optimistic. But Ryan had muscular dystrophy, and the degenerative process was so advanced in him that he never walked, never played ball, never did so many of the things his friends did.

He wanted to, though, because he never saw himself in terms of being different or disabled. Which was why the summer camps he attended were so important to him. All the kids there had pretty much the same abilities he had, and the fact that swimming or horseback-riding was a little different for them did not make a difference. For the time Ryan and his friends were at camp they got to be kids, doing kid things like all their other friends did.

Ryan wasn't given a lot of time on this earth, but he exceeded all expectations—went to college, became a high school teacher, travelled the world. Much of this independence he gained through his camp experiences, and because of what I saw resulting from those summer weeks, where his differences didn't matter, I decided to write about a camp much the same as Ryan attended—where kids, no matter what their condition, are allowed to be kids.

Did you go to camp when you were a kid? What kinds of memories do you have? I went to camp every summer and loved it. I didn't fall in love there, the way Keera and Reid do in my story. But I remember some pretty good summer crushes, some mighty cute boys, and a lot of great fun. *Definitely* some great fun (and my first kiss!).

Wishing you health, happiness, and great summer camp memories!

Dianne

PS I'd love to hear about your summer camp memories. Please feel free to check out my website at www.Dianne-Drake.com, and contact me through that. Or e-mail me at DianneDrake@earthlink.net. I'm on Facebook too, at Facebook.com/DianneDrakeAuthor

A CHILD TO HEAL
THEIR HEARTS

BY
DIANNE DRAKE

First published in Great Britain 2013
by Mills & Boon, an imprint of Harlequin (UK) Limited.
Harlequin (UK) Limited, Eton House,
18-24 Paradise Road, Richmond, Surrey TW9 1SR

© Dianne Despain 2013

ISBN: 978 0 263 89913 9

Harlequin (UK) policy is to use papers that are natural, renewable and recyclable products and made from wood grown in sustainable forests. The logging and manufacturing process conform to the legal environmental regulations of the country of origin.

Printed and bound in Spain
by Blackprint CPI, Barcelona

Now that her children have left home, **Dianne Drake** is finally finding the time to do some of the things she adores—gardening, cooking, reading, shopping for antiques. Her absolute passion in life, however, is adopting abandoned and abused animals. Right now Dianne and her husband Joel have a little menagerie of three dogs and two cats, but that's always subject to change. A former symphony orchestra member, Dianne now attends the symphony as a spectator several times a month and, when time permits, takes in an occasional football, basketball, or hockey game.

Recent titles by Dianne Drake:

P.S. YOU'RE A DADDY
REVEALING THE REAL DR ROBINSON
THE DOCTOR'S LOST-AND-FOUND HEART
NO. 1 DAD IN TEXAS
THE RUNAWAY NURSE
FIREFIGHTER WITH A FROZEN HEART
THE DOCTOR'S REASON TO STAY**
FROM BROODING BOSS TO ADORING DAD
THE BABY WHO STOLE THE DOCTOR'S HEART*

**New York Hospital Heartthrobs*
Mountain Village Hospital

CHAPTER ONE

"COMING!" KEERA'S sleep-scratchy voice barely cleared the bedroom door and there was no way the person outside on her front porch could hear her. But she didn't really care. This was *her* time. Off work.

She wasn't on call, and after tomorrow she had no hospital obligations for the next week. A few days off after an entire year on. Blessed vacation time for eating, sleeping, reading. Most of all, quiet time to herself. No one to intrude, no one to disturb her. Time alone was all she had on the schedule and she adamantly didn't want to be disturbed before her holiday started. But as chief of cardiac surgery, she didn't always get what she wanted. Case in point, someone was knocking right now, and rather vigorously at that.

"OK, OK. Give me a minute," she grumbled on a weary sigh, the sentiment directed more to the neon green clock light blinking acrimoniously at her from the nightstand than to anything or anyone else.

She blinked back at it, wanted to throw a shoe at it when she saw it was telling her the time was ten after two. And she'd only been in bed since twenty after one. Meaning she'd had fifty full minutes of sleep.

"Figures," she grunted as another knock jolted her out of her blearies. Then another knock, louder this time. Last time this had happened to her, it had been the National Guard come to fetch her in the middle of a torrential storm. *"Hospital's on emergency alert, Dr. Murphy. Don't want you driving in this because of the conditions, so we've come to take you in."* Yep, that had been quite a night, being hefted up into the back of a military helicopter and jostled around fallen trees and power lines.

But tonight there was no rain. No storm or adverse condition of any kind going on. And as Keera's mind started to clear, she began ticking off the various reasons someone might be doing exactly what they were doing. Worst-case scenario—full-out disaster that wasn't weather-related. Best-case scenario—emergency surgery waiting. But why not simply call her, like they always did?

Maybe they had. Maybe she'd slept through it. "I *said* I'm coming," she shouted, cinching her robe as she plodded out to the entry hall. "Identify yourself, please," she shouted, even though a glimpse through the peephole revealed the uniform of a police officer. "And show me some identification."

"Will do, Miss Murphy," the man out there shouted.

Miss Murphy. After fast-tracking her way through medical school and all the other stages that had preceded cardiac surgeon, that's what it all boiled down to, wasn't it? Unmarried doctor, unmarried *miss*… Successful at career, unsuccessful at life. It was pretty much everything that defined her.

Keera pushed her long red hair back from her face, and looked out again. Saw what she required from the first officer.

"Officer Carla James," she said, obliging Keera with a sight of her ID. Short woman, slightly rounded, definitely hiding behind the taller officer.

"And Officer Brian Hutchinson," the taller one added,

bending down to Keera's peephole so she'd get a good wide-angle view of his face then his badge. "Would you please open the door?"

"Is it medical business?" she shouted at them, as she unlatched the first of three safety chains then finally pulled back the dead bolt. A little extra precaution as a result of living alone.

"No, ma'am, it's not," Officer Hutchinson said, stepping forward as soon as the door opened to him. He held out his leather wallet for her to match his photo with his face. Then tucked it away when she'd nodded her satisfaction. "I'm sorry to say it's personal."

That's when the first grain of relief shot through her. Keera Murphy didn't have a personal life. Everything about her was medicine. "How? I mean, what?"

Officer James chose that moment to step out from behind Hutchinson, and the only thing Keera saw was the bundle in her arms. "I'm sorry. I don't understand." Were they bringing her a patient? A child? No. This was a mistake. Didn't make sense. They were at the wrong house, or had the wrong person. That had to be it. They wanted the Keera Murphy who was a pediatrician, if there was such a person, and she was the Keera Murphy who did cardiac surgery.

"I'm sorry to say, there's no easy way to do this," Officer Hutchinson continued. "But earlier this evening your husband and a yet unidentified passenger were killed in a single vehicle crash off Mountain Canyon Road. Your daughter was thrown free, and escaped without injury. We did have her checked at a clinic near there, and except for some scrapes and bruises she's fine. In shock, I think, because she's not talking, maybe a little lethargic due to the trauma. But the doc who looked at her said she was basically good."

"I'm glad, but this is a mistake because I'm not married." Keera took a step backwards, braced herself against the wall. "Divorced. No children."

"Kevin Murphy," Hutchinson continued. "Kevin Joseph Murphy, ma'am. Your husband, according to some legal papers we found at the scene. House deed, this address."

"But we're not... Haven't been..." She shut her eyes, trying to focus. Kevin was dead? Their marriage had been a real stinker and their divorce nasty in epic proportions, but she wouldn't have wished this on him. "You're sure?" she finally managed.

"Yes, ma'am. We have a full identification on your husband but not his passenger. We were hoping..."

Keera glanced at the officer holding the child, wondering why they'd brought her here. Wondering if this was the child who... It had to be. Who else could she be but the child he'd fathered while they had still been married? "Maybe the passenger is his *second* wife. Melanie, Melodie, something like that." Or the one after her, if there'd already been another as Kevin seemed to have his women in fast succession. "Melania, that's her name. Melania." Keera's head was spinning now the information was finally beginning to sink in. Kevin was dead, most likely along with his second wife. And their child... "She's not mine," she said.

"But you were listed as Mr. Murphy's wife and next of kin, so we assumed—"

"Wrong assumption," she said, cutting him off. "Old information. My husband and I divorced a few months ago, the papers you found were probably from part of the agreement." Or, in their case, disagreement. "He called several days ago, said he had some final papers for me to sign, and that child..." She shook her head. "Part of his second marriage." Kevin's secret to keep, along with his mistress.

"Then we have a problem," Carla James said, "because we have nowhere to take the child for the night."

A little girl, she'd been told. Keera had never actually seen her. Hadn't ever wanted to see her. Didn't want to see her now, even though that was about to change. "Surely, there's a foster-home with an opening. Or some kind of contingency in place for situations like this one?"

Both police officers shook their heads.

"Social services?" Hopeful question with an answer she'd already guessed.

"That would be me," a perky young woman said from behind Officer James. "My name is Consuela Martinez, and I'm the temporary case manager assigned to Megan. And right now I don't have a contingency plan that would be in the child's best interests. We were hoping her family—"

"But I'm not her family," Keera interrupted.

Consuela stepped out in plain sight, the yellow of the porch light giving her more of a jaundiced look than it should. And just like that Keera switched to doctor mode, her mind ticking off various conditions that came with a yellow tinge…one of the reasons Kevin had strayed, *he claimed*. Too much doctor too much of the time. Sadly, she hadn't had an argument to counter his because, in the end, she *had* loved her medicine more than she'd loved her husband or their marriage.

"Look, I know there's a contingency plan," Keera said. "When a child is involved there's always a contingency plan." It was said without conviction because she really didn't know that to be the case. But she hoped it was, or else…

"You're right. Usually there is. Except right now. Every spot we have for someone Megan's age and developmental stage is filled," the case worker continued. "But I can have a callout to other agencies in other areas by morning, or we might be able to shift a few children to other situations, and after that—"

"Are you taking flucloxacillin, by any chance, Consuela?" Keera interrupted, so totally *not* wanting to hear that Megan had no place to go tonight.

Consuela looked confused. For that matter, so did both police officers. "Um, yes. I am. For an outer ear infection. Why?"

"You might want to call your doctor first thing in the morning and mention that you're having an adverse reaction to the drug. Nothing serious, so don't be alarmed. But it's worth noting." And that didn't change the problem at hand, as there was still a child bundled in Officer James's arms who needed a place to stay. "Sorry," she said. "Force of habit. Part of my job is paying attention to the details, and I've been told I can go overboard about it."

"It's good to know you're conscientious, Doctor," Officer Hutchinson said, "but it's two-thirty, and we're not getting any closer to figuring out what to do with—"

"With my ex-husband's child." It was an irony coming back to slap her hard. This was his secret child, the one he'd told her he'd fathered but had only told her on the child's first birthday. His first devastating confession, followed by how much he loved the baby's mother, how he wanted a divorce, wanted to keep their house for his new family... But none of that was Megan's fault, was it? "You're sure there's really no place for her to go tonight?"

"The county home," Consuela said, "which I try to avoid when I can, especially for children so young. It's a large facility, too many children. The younger ones get... overlooked."

"It's an—"

"An institution, ma'am," Officer James volunteered. "In

the traditional sense. But if you're rejecting the child, it's our only recourse, because I can't stand on your doorstep all night, holding her."

"No, of course you can't," Keera said, taking a step backwards as she felt her resolve start to melt. Another step, pause…taking a moment to gird her resolve. Then another backwards step, and finally the gesture to enter her home. And as Officer James passed her, Keera took her first good look at Megan, and if it weren't for the fact that the room was filled with people…strangers, she would have fallen to her knees. Would have cried. The lump in her throat started to choke her, and the light feeling in her head caused the room to spin. "Please, lay her on the sofa. I can sit up in here with her, she shouldn't be alone." *Shouldn't be in an institution!* No child should ever be in an institution.

Keera glanced at Consuela, who'd stopped at the mirror in the entry hall and was staring at her yellow-tinted complexion. "But this is only until morning," she warned the social worker. "If you don't have a placement for her before I leave for the hospital, in exactly three hours, you'll find her in the daycare center.

"Oh, and, Consuela, I can't look after her longer than what I've said. I'm not good with children. They don't respond to me, and outside normal medical situations I wouldn't know how to respond if they did. So, come morning, do you understand me? My early surgery will be over by ten, followed by routine rounds, and I don't want to go into my rounds knowing I still have a child to worry about."

It made her sound unpleasant, like a bully or, worse… heartless. Which wasn't at all what she'd intended. But how did a person go about dealing with a situation like this? She'd just taken in the child who had caused the final curtain to drop on her marriage, and she wasn't sure there was a proper way to deal with that.

"So, before you go, do we know if she has any allergies?" Kevin had been allergic to shellfish. "Or medical conditions that require attention…or medication?"

Consuela, who'd finally torn herself away from the mirror, shook her head. "Her doctor is Reid Adams, and his practice is in a little town called Sugar Creek, Tennessee. About an hour or so west of here. But we haven't been able to get in touch with him yet. He's at camp."

"Camp?" Keera asked.

"Youth camp, for kids recovering from leukemia and all the associated conditions. He's the camp physician, I've been told. And I do have a call in for him." Consuela stepped around Keera, who made no move to help Officer James settle Megan on the sofa. "And, Dr. Murphy… she's a good child. Very quiet. She won't cause you any problems."

No, the child wouldn't. Not now, anyway, because Keera's problems were in the past. And while little Megan hadn't caused them, she was a result of them. "Noon at the very latest. Please find your contingency plan by noon."

Ten minutes later, when the house was quiet again, Keera settled into the chair across from the sofa and simply stared at the child. Lovely little girl. Blonde hair, like Kevin's. Probably blue eyes like his, too. Sadly, there was so much turmoil for one little life. Poor thing. Her heart did go out to Megan for so many reasons.

"It's good that you don't have to understand any of this," Keera whispered to the child, while she pulled her feet up under herself, preparing to spend the rest of her night right there, looking after the girl. "But you're going to be fine. You're a beautiful little girl, and everything's going to be fine."

* * *

"I'm sorry, Doctor, but I really don't have anything to tell you." Reid Adams tossed the ball into the grass then stood back to watch the stampede of children go after it. No matter what else was going on in his life, coming to camp was always a highlight. "I'd have to look at her records before I could say anything, but I'm not in my office this week and—"

"Then find someone who can do it for you," Keera snapped, then hastily added, "Look, I'm sorry I sound so grumpy, but…"

"Normally, if someone sounds grumpy, they're grumpy," Reid said, stepping behind the large oak tree as two little girls came running in his direction. Black hair, dark eyes, dark skin. Hispanic beauties, and the lights of his life. His reason for existing wrapped up in a couple of very energetic little girls, aged five and seven. "And I think your situation with Megan would make a lot of people grumpy if it happened to them. No relatives turn up yet?"

"An elderly aunt who refused the child, as well as some male cousins the social worker thought weren't suitable. Apparently there are other family members being contacted, but I may have the child through the afternoon, and I'd feel better knowing about her health situation."

He liked her voice. A little husky, but not so much she sounded like a three-packs-a-day smoker. More like bedroom-sultry husky…an image that caused him to blink hard, clear his throat and, more than anything else, remind him that this was a kids' camp and he was surrounded by a bunch of kids who didn't need a distracted counselor.

"Daddy," five-year-old Allie squealed, as Reid sidled around the tree, only to be waylaid by seven-year-old Emmie, coming at him from the other side.

"I found him first," Emmie shouted.

"Did not," Allie argued, latching onto Reid's leg. "I got him first."

"You both got me first," he declared.

"Excuse me," Keera said. "Dr. Adams?"

"Sorry about that," he said, chuckling. "But my daughters are persistent, and they won't take no for an answer when we're playing. Not that I'd ever want them to. So, getting back to Megan Murphy. I've seen her once, I think, and nothing stands out. But it's a new practice, I'm barely settled in, and I don't know enough about any of my patients yet to even recognize them, or their parents, on the street. Sorry about that, because I'd like to be more help. But let me call either Beau Alexander or his wife, Deanna. They're covering my practice this week and they might know something. Or be able to see what's in the records." Pause.

"Girls, girls! Stay away from that fence! That's the rule. You've been told if you go near the fence, you'll get a time out with your first warning, and broccoli with your dinner with your second warning."

"You punish the children by threatening them with broccoli?" Keera asked. "I'd think that would be a healthy choice. Something you'd encourage them to eat."

"It is, but most kids come naturally equipped hating broccoli, so I use that to my advantage. Then, by the end of the camp session, we'll have introduced them to a couple of ways broccoli can taste really yummy… Excuse me, I have the younger group here this week. When I mention broccoli to older kids, I usually use the term delicious. And the thing is, the majority of these children will leave here and ask their parents for broccoli. Just an FYI—raw with dip works great!"

"Raw or cooked, you're a magician, Dr. Adams, if you get them liking broccoli."

"Nope, just a single dad who's figured it out. If it works with my two, it'll work with anybody's kid. Anyway... Angelica, Rodney! Take off your shoes *and* your socks before you go wading in the creek! Both socks, Rodney."

"Look, I appreciate your time, Dr. Adams, but—"

"Reid. Call me Reid."

"Reid. I'm sorry for sounding so grumpy, or frazzled, or whatever you want to call it, but I'm not good with children, don't know if I even like them so much, and I really don't want to be responsible for one, even if it's only for a few more hours. I was hoping...actually, I don't know what I was hoping for. But you clearly have your hands full with your camp kids, so I'm going let you go. But before I do, could you answer one more question for me?"

"Got time for two, if they're quick." Truth was, he wasn't sure he wanted to hang up. Keera Murphy sounded nice, except for the part where she wasn't fond of children. In his life that was definitely a problem. But she wasn't in his life, so it didn't matter. "So go ahead."

"Megan's two, and she's not... She's still in diapers. I had her in hospital daycare all morning and the ladies working there said she made no attempt to go to the bathroom or even ask someone to take her."

"Does she speak?"

"No, but that could be the trauma."

"She's had a full battery of tests?"

"Everything we could think of."

"Then she's probably just reacting to her circumstances. Once things are normal around her again I'm sure the diapers can come off. And if she's not totally trained, it's perfectly natural for children that age to be a little resistant. But if you have other concerns, please feel free..." He spun around in time to catch Emmie ready to lob him with a big red water balloon. He was fast enough to dodge it, but in trying for the evasive maneuver he dropped his phone. By the time he'd manage to pick it back up, Keera Murphy had hung up.

"Who was that, Daddy?" Allie asked him. Now she was sneaking up, hiding what he guessed was also a filled water balloon behind her back. So, he could take it like a man or, actually, like a daddy, and let his youngest have her turn at dousing Daddy, or he could spin and run like crazy. After all, he was well over six feet tall, considered well muscled by some. Legs that had helped him finish in the pack at a few marathons. So if he couldn't outrun a little girl… "She was a doctor."

"Who takes care of little kids, like you do?" Allie asked. The expression on her face was so determined, he knew what he had to do.

"No, not that kind of doctor, sweetheart." He braced himself for the hit. "Remember when we talked about what having surgery means?" OK, so most parents weren't quite as forthright as he was in his child-rearing ideas, but he didn't believe in lying, not even when it was about something Allie probably wouldn't even understand and definitely didn't need to know.

"Where they have to make a zipper so they can see your insides?"

He chuckled. "Actually, yes." Which meant she did listen to him. Music to the ears of a long-suffering parent. "She's the kind of doctor who makes the zipper."

He thought back to the conversation with Keera. Strained, at best. Maybe more like totally stressed out. Someone he pictured as nervous. Someone he also pictured as… One momentary distraction was all it took, and Reid Adams fell victim to his daughter, who landed the perfectly placed water balloon center chest. "Got me," he shouted, dropping to the ground, where five or six other children converged on him and bombarded him with water balloons the way his own daughters had done.

"No fair," he shouted while laughs and squeals muffled any protest he wanted to make. Not that he really wanted to protest. This was part of his fun. What meant the most to him now was thinking about how his daughters would be exhilarated, and knowing that his two little conspirators had led a group of normally sedentary kids into an adventure was, probably, the most fun of all.

Then he wondered about Dr. Keera Murphy. Would she have seen any of this as fun? Or worthless, as she wasn't a big one for children? More than that, why did it even matter to him? And why did he make a mental note to do a little Internet surfing on her when he had time?

"No more water balloons," he shouted, trying to stand up. But to no avail. As he rose to his knees, a whole new group of water ballooners swarmed him, loaded down with filled balloons of every size, color and shape imaginable. He barely had enough time to cover his face before the fun began.

"I know what I said, Dr. Murphy, and I've got a line on someone who might take her later tonight or some time tomorrow, if there's nobody else available. But Mrs. Blanchard prefers her wards to be toilet trained, and as Megan isn't, I'm not sure she'll get all the attention she needs."

They were sitting in the parents' waiting room across from the hospital daycare center. A very cheerful place. Lots of bright yellows and oranges, like they were tying the conventional child stimuli colors into their parents. This was only the second time Keera had ever been there. The first had been that morning, when she'd left Megan in the able care of Dolores Anderson, the director. "She could be traumatized."

"Maybe, and if that's the case, I'm wondering if a pediatric hospital ward might be the best place for her temporarily."

"Seriously, you want to stick her in a hospital?"

No, that was not acceptable. While she didn't have any strong urges toward the child, she wasn't some cold-hearted dungeon master who wanted to lock all the untrained kiddies away until they potty trained themselves. This was a child who needed attention, not isolation, and so far all of Consuela's ideas seemed more like isolation.

"Look, just keep trying with Mrs. Blanchard, OK? If she won't take Megan, maybe she'll have a suggestion about who can."

"We'll work it out, Doctor. I promise, that's all I've been doing today."

Consuela was deliberately not making eye contact with Keera, trying to keep her gaze focused on anything else, and Keera accepted that. She'd probably do the same thing if she found herself in that same spot. But what Consuela didn't understand was that so far today childcare had been a breeze because she'd had the help of the whole hospital daycare staff there to get her through it.

Tomorrow was another story. It was her day off—the start of her week off, in fact. And that's when the reading commenced with a whole stack of medical journals she'd had for a year or more. Nowhere in those plans was there room for a toddler.

"I'm not criticizing you, and I hope you don't think that I was. But I grew up in the foster-care system. A lot of it in institutions, and it's horrible. Being passed off from one place to another, never knowing where you might end up next. I never got adopted because I was older when I went into the system, so I was in a grand total of nine different homes and three different institutions, all before the age of eighteen. And, no, I wasn't a good child because of that." She closed her eyes, fighting back those memories.

"This child doesn't need that kind of trauma in her life." As much as she'd disliked Kevin by the end of their marriage, Keera knew he would have been a very good father. A doting daddy. Megan didn't deserve to go from that to cold indifference, which was what would happen if she was sent to an institution. Or even the wrong foster-family.

"It's not always a traumatic situation, Doctor. We have very good caregivers."

"Yes, I'm sure you do, and I admire people who would take on the responsibility. Right now, though, Megan needs more that what you're able to find her, and I know that's not your fault. But it's not her fault either. Yet she's the one who's going to be bounced around or institutionalized."

And she was waging the battle with the wrong person. She knew that. But the right person—the one who should have made arrangements for Megan in the event something like this happened—was dead. True to Kevin's form, he hadn't thought about the practical things. Hadn't when they'd been married, hadn't after they were divorced, and now his daughter was paying the price.

"I'm sorry about your childhood, Doctor, and I understand your frustration but, like I said, I'm doing my best. There aren't any distant relatives suited to take her, or who even want her, for that matter, so I have to come up with another plan. But you've got to understand that in the short term Megan might have to go to a hospital pediatric ward, a group home or even the county home. It's not what I want to do but what I may have to do if you can't or won't keep her for a little while longer."

"In the meantime…" Resignation crept in a little too

quickly, but maybe she saw something of herself in Megan. Abandoned child. It was hard to get past that. "If I keep her a day or two, that doesn't mean I want to be a temporary guardian or any other kind of custodial figure. It simply means I'll feed and clothe her while you continue looking for a better situation."

"Which I'll do," Consuela promised.

"Good. So now I've got to go to the grocery and buy a few things a toddler would eat. Maybe pick up some clothes, toys…" OK, so she was relating to the situation but not to Megan herself. It was the best she could do. Better than most people would do, she thought as she bundled up the child and took her to the car. This was an honest effort, and it kept the child out of all those awful places Keera knew so intimately. Shuddered even thinking about them. Dark places, bad for children…

While having children had never been part of her plan—past, present or future—there'd been a time when she'd needed what Megan needed now, and no one had reached out to her. So how could she refuse?

"Megan, did you have a good day today?" she asked as they wended their way through the hospital corridors on her way to her car. "Play with lots of nice toys? Meet new people? Conquer any toddler nations?"

In response, Megan laid her head against Keera's shoulder and sighed.

"You're congested," Keera said, listening to the slight rattling she could hear coming from the girl's lungs. Immediately in doctor mode, she veered off into one of the pediatric exam cubicles, pulled her stethoscope from her pocket and listened. Nothing sounded serious, but the fact remained that the child had something going on that needed to be attended to…sooner, not later. And every thought in her went to Reid Adams.

CHAPTER TWO

"IT'S OK, MEGAN," she said, barely creeping along the mountain highway. "We'll be there soon, and Dr. Adams will take good care of you." She hoped so, even though she wasn't sure the message had gotten through because he hadn't called her back. Something about mountains and cellphone interference.

"You've seen him before, and he's very good." Not that the sleeping child cared. But Keera did. She wanted some familiarity for Megan, and Reid Adams was the closest thing she could think of. And maybe, just maybe, he'd have a solution for the child's situation. "We're not far away now, so you just sleep there, and when you wake up things will be better. I promise."

What was she promising, though? What, really, could a trip to an isolated camp in the mountains in the middle of the night do for Megan? Nothing. That's what! But it made Keera feel better. Feel like she was doing something rather than simply sitting around waiting for something to happen or, worse, doing the wrong thing. Reid Adams was all about children, he had children. And for some strange reason, he seemed like her best port in the storm. A beacon of light.

"He'll know what to do," she reassured the sleeping child. "Yes, I'm sure of it." Because if he didn't...well,

Keera didn't want to think about the alternative, since it wasn't acceptable. That was something she knew in profound ways no child should ever have to know. Confusion, fear and long, empty days and nights when the futility threatened to eat you alive. "He'll fix you up, and he'll help me help you, too."

Those were mighty big expectations for one pediatrician to fulfill, but it's all Keera had to cling to. Reid Adams had to come through for both their sakes. He just had to!

He wasn't sure who she was, but for some reason he thought he could wager a pretty good guess. Carrying a child in her arms, she was trying to make her way up the dirt path without stumbling, and she was quite obviously not a woman of the woods. Determined, though. With the scowl of a mighty huntress set across one of the softest, prettiest faces he'd ever seen in his life.

Which was what had brought Keera Murphy to mind. She'd tracked him down and she was bringing him the child. He wasn't sure why, wasn't even sure that he liked the idea that the huntress had set her sights on him. But something about a woman who would trudge all the way out here in the middle of the night just to find him did fascinate him.

"You would be Dr. Murphy?" he asked, as she approached the porch of his cabin.

"I would be. And this is Megan Murphy. She's sick. Since nobody knows her, nobody knows a thing about her, well, with you being her physician and all, I thought you'd be the best one to take a look."

"You couldn't find another physician closer to you? Or even track down one of my colleagues?"

"You didn't get my phone call?"

"Mountains and cellphones aren't always a good combination, even in this day and age. Reception out here is spotty, which is why we still rely on the landline."

"Well, I called because I hoped she'd remember you. With everything she's gone through, I thought that would be good. Maybe it doesn't matter, but…" Keera started up the wooden steps and Reid took the child from her arms, immediately seeing how sick she was.

"How long has she been this way?" he asked, turning and nearly running into his cabin.

"Just the last few hours. She'd been getting progressively sicker and I wasn't too worried about it at first, but when I listened to her chest a little while ago, the congestion had more than doubled from earlier and her temperature had elevated two degrees."

He laid Megan carefully on the sofa then dashed into the next room after his medical bag.

"Well, I hope I didn't do the wrong thing bringing her here." She shrugged. "And I'm sorry for the intrusion. Maybe I panicked a little." Panicked because she'd known what would happen if she'd taken Megan to the hospital. The system would have gotten her. As much as she didn't want the child, she also didn't want the child to end up in the system, which was what would have happened because a trip to Emergency tonight would have started that process. "I didn't know what else to do."

"You followed your instinct. Did what you believed was best. It's not a bad thing, Keera." He took a quick blood-pressure reading, followed by the rest of Megan's vitals, then pulled off his stethoscope and laid it aside.

It was a simple action yet so sexy. And she wanted to kick herself for noticing. "I may have overreacted, but—"

"Look, I don't know the dynamics here. Don't know why social services left the child with you when, clearly, she's not your responsibility. Don't know why you avoided a quick trip to an emergency room rather than driving all the way out here. But I'm not going to ask. We all have our reasons for the crazy things we do, and I don't mean crazy in a literal sense but more from a point of observation. Seems crazy to me because I don't know what makes you tick, but obviously it doesn't seem crazy to you because you understand the situation. So as far as I'm concerned, it's all good."

"I appreciate that," she said sincerely. "Thank you."

"Don't thank me yet. I want to keep Megan for a day or so. It's probably a slight upper respiratory infection, although I want to make sure before I let her go as I don't think she's up to another trip back with you so soon. So I'd like to keep her in the infirmary here for a little while, if you don't mind. It's empty and I can quarantine her there just to make sure the other kids don't come in contact with her. Then I'll get her hydrated and start her on some medication to make her feel better." He frowned. "Unless you'd rather admit her to a local hospital because she is a little dehydrated. Your choice."

No choice. This was where Megan had to be, at least for the night. "And the infirmary is…?"

He pointed to a door at the rear of the living room. "Through the kitchen, out the door, first building you see beyond my cabin. The clinic is on the other side of the compound."

"Why do you keep them separated?"

"These kids are very susceptible to illness. Don't want sickness anywhere near regular medical duties."

"Makes sense."

"Also, I bought the camp as is. Didn't have one place large enough to house both the clinic and infirmary. Anyway, there's always someone on duty. Usually me, sometimes Betsy, the camp nurse, who stays in the cabin adjacent to this one. We alternate nights taking call.

"As far as the infirmary, I think you may have to help a bit there because Betsy's pregnant and I don't let her near the sick kids. Which means it's basically you and me, and I do have a volunteer who isn't medical but who had leukemia when she was a kid and enjoys helping out where she can."

"You need to know I'm not good at pediatrics."

"Maybe not, but I don't have a lot of options if we're going to keep Megan here. Like I said, there's always the hospital…"

An unacceptable choice. That was her first thought. Her second was that she could leave Megan here, go home and let Consuela, the social worker, deal with the rest of it. This was certainly her chance to step aside and know Megan was in good hands, but something inside her was stopping her from taking it. "So you want me basically quarantined with her?"

"Not quarantined as in locked up. We have a guest cabin. Nothing fancy, but a place to sleep for the rest of the night, if you want it, while I watch Megan. Then in the morning we can work out the schedule."

"Maybe she'll be ready to travel in the morning." And maybe in the morning Consuela would call her and tell her she'd found a perfect placement. Maybe even a good family who would eventually adopt Megan. One who'd been on the waiting list, praying for a beautiful two-year-old girl. Sure, it was a long shot, she knew that. But it was also a very nice dream—a dream she'd never had for her own.

"That's possible," he said. "But unlikely. In the meantime, you look like you're due for a few hours of sleep."

Yes, she did want that sleep. More now that he'd mentioned it. Hypnotic effect—her eyelids were getting heavy.

"Definitely no hospital, so I guess it looks like I'm staying. I think I'll talk to Megan for a minute then I'll take you up on that cabin. Oh, and, Reid, I really am sorry to put you through this. If there's anything I can do…"

"How about I carry her to the infirmary then you can tuck her in while I run over to the girls' dorm and check on my daughters?" He smiled. "They may think they're getting away from Dad, but it's not happening. Anyway, one last kiss goodnight while you settle Megan in, then I'll point you in the direction of the guest cabin and you're on your own. Oh, and breakfast is at eight. Big white building in the middle of the complex. Meals are prompt, but if you sleep in, I always have cereal and milk in my own kitchen."

He was tall, a bit lanky. Wore wire-rimmed glasses, needed a haircut. She liked his scraggly look, though. Light brown hair, slightly curly, slightly over his collar. Slight dimple in his chin. And, oh, those blue eyes. Wow, they were perceptive. So much so they almost scared her. "I don't sleep much so I'll be good to grab something with everybody else."

"I'm just saying…" he said, scooping Megan into his arms and heading out to the infirmary.

Keera opened the door to the infirmary, saw exactly four beds. It was a tidy space, not large, not lush. Just basic. "Do many of your kids get sick?"

"Not really. By the point in their recovery that they're allowed to come to camp, they're usually pretty far along in the whole process, with all kinds of specialists making the determination whether or not they're ready for the whole camping experience. In other words, barring normal things like colds and flu, they're usually doing pretty well."

"Well, it sounds like you're doing important work. So

don't you think the owners would put a little more effort into the medical facility that might have to treat those kids? I mean, this place will suffice, but it could certainly stand some updates and expansion." After Reid laid Megan in the bed, Keera pulled up the blanket to cover her. "Closer to the clinic would be nice, too, to save you some steps."

"Are you always like this?"

"What?"

"Outspoken. Opinionated. Whatever you want to call it." Grabbing a fresh digital thermometer from the drawer in the stand next to the bed, he pulled it from its wrapper, punched the button and waited for it to calibrate. "Something to say pretty much on every subject." The thermometer end went under Megan's tongue the same time his eyes went to Keera's. "I'm right about that, aren't I?"

"It's been said." Amongst a lot worse things. "I'm a cardiac surgeon in a large hospital, and—"

"I know who you are."

"How?"

"Internet search."

"When?"

"Earlier. After you called. You sounded like someone who might come back to haunt me later on, so I decided to read up. Good thing I did, because…"

She smiled, almost apologetically but not quite. "Because I came back to haunt you."

The thermometer beeped and Reid pulled it out and read it. Then shook his head. "One hundred three and a couple of decimal points." Immediately, he pulled up Megan's eyelids, took a look. She responded by whimpering and trying to jerk away from him.

"I talked to Beau a couple hours ago. He'd looked at the records we have for her, saw nothing significant. In fact, the only time she's been to the office was when her parents first moved to Sugar Creek, and they were establishing me as their pediatrician. I gave her a preliminary exam, sort of as a baseline, and there was nothing remarkable. She's developed properly for a child her age, and according to her parents there's no history of any chronic illness or condition.

"But that's me taking their word for it because they never had her medical records transferred to us, and there's no mention of a former pediatrician, so right now we really know very little. Which means we're coming into her care pretty much blind."

"Trust me, blind is bad."

"I get the feeling that has nothing to do with Megan."

"Actually, it has everything to do with her. But not in the medical sense."

Pulling out his stethoscope, Reid listened to the child's chest, her heart, her tummy then pulled out his earpieces. "Didn't hear anything more remarkable than what you probably heard. Bilateral congestion, wheezing." He shrugged. "Indicative of any number of things. Which means I'm going to need lab work that I'm not equipped to do here."

"Did it before I came here. Results should be in by morning. And I have her X-ray in the car."

"You come prepared. Too bad all my patients don't come in with all their tests already done."

"Like I told you, I don't know a thing about children. Don't treat them, don't operate on them, don't want to. But getting everything done beforehand seemed logical."

"Well, even though you've complicated my life by bringing her here, you've made my complication easier."

"You're not supposed to treat anybody who's not at camp? Is that the problem? Because I can talk to the owner or director. Apologize. Make the appropriate donation for her care, if that's what's needed to make this better."

"Actually, I own the camp so I can do what I want. And donations are always welcome. But just so you'll know, she's got the start of a rash on her stomach, so I think she's probably coming down with measles, most likely in the early part of its three or four days of infectivity. Meaning while she's in here I can't have other children anywhere near her. So if somebody else needs the facility…" He shrugged. "I'll treat her here for now, certainly for the night, and we'll do the best we can with what we have. But I can't make any promises beyond that. Fair enough?"

"More than fair," she said, grateful for what he was offering.

"Have you had measles, by the way?"

"Not that I remember. But I don't remember a lot of my childhood, so I don't really know."

"Vaccinated?"

"That, I was. Required in school." When she had gone, which hadn't been too often. "Could this be something else, though? An allergic reaction of some sort?" Reid Adams was an acclaimed pediatrician—she'd done her Internet surfing as well. So it was highly unlikely he'd make a mistake of a pretty basic diagnosis. Still, an allergic reaction resulting in a rash beat measles any day, so she was keeping her fingers crossed.

"If I were a betting man, I'd bet she's going to have a full-blown rash by this time tomorrow."

"And you still want to keep her? Especially with all the other children being so susceptible? I mean, I could take her to a hotel someplace close, so she wouldn't have to suffer that long drive back tonight."

"She's too congested to move her any place, if we don't have to. It would risk complications. And she has to be sick somewhere, doesn't she? Seeing that you're not in favor of taking her to the hospital, which would really be the only place I'd approve sending her..."

"If she absolutely needs to be in a hospital, that's what I'll do. I just have personal preferences about not leaving an already abandoned child in an institution." Keera looked down at the girl, and her heart clutched. Poor thing, she didn't deserve cold detachment, but that's all Keera was capable of giving. She knew her limitations.

"She's not my child, but I want what's best for her, and while I know you're a pediatrician and you'll disagree with me, I don't happen to think it would be in a hospital. And I don't say that lightly as I work in a hospital."

"Couldn't agree with you more about hospitals." He pushed a strand of hair away from Megan's face then stood. "Don't like them myself if they're not necessary. Look, I really do need to go say goodnight to my girls, then I'll be back to put an IV in her and give her some fluids to keep her hydrated. I think that will be easier than trying to get her to drink anything right now. It'll only take me a couple of minutes..."

"I'm really sorry about this," Keera said, feeling the need to apologize over and over because of what she was doing to Reid and his camp. It was an inconvenience at very best and a danger at worst.

"She's sick. Bringing her all the way out here might not have been my first choice, but it's a difficult situation. Can't say I understand your decisions, but I'm not going to argue about them. So why the worried look?"

"I'm still concerned about exposing the other kids. I didn't think about that before I came here, and I feel terrible."

"See, the thing about being a pediatrician is you're always in contact with something that's highly contagious.

In my office, I actually have separate waiting areas for kids with something *catchy*, as I like to call it. They never go to the general waiting room, never come near one of the other kids. Bottom line, I'm cautious and it works. So does the fact that we're surrounded by the great outdoors so there aren't any environmental factors that would help promote exposure."

"You sure?"

He nodded, smiled. "Sure."

"Do you have a solution for my fear of children as well?"

"Afraid of children, yet you're a good doctor."

"Definitely afraid of children. Don't know what to do for them, or with them. I was a nervous wreck every time I had to rotate through Pediatrics when I was a resident."

"Somehow I don't picture you being a nervous wreck about anything."

"I appreciate the compliment, but I'm serious about children. They're not my strength. Speaking of which, there's something you should know about Megan. And it's not really her so much as the whole situation. But only because you're her doctor."

He motioned Keera to the door. "Tell me as you walk me out."

She did, then stopped at the door as he stepped out into the night. "Without dragging out all the dirty laundry, what you need to know is that Keera is the child my husband conceived with another woman while he and I were still married, still going through the motions that made it look like a good marriage. We had our share of problems, like all couples do, but I didn't know he was cheating on me. Didn't even know his affair produced a child until she was a year old, and he was wanting out of our marriage so he could invest himself fully in his other family. That was a year ago. Haven't seen him since except across the table at the lawyer's office. And I'd never seen the child until…"

"Yet here you are with her, going above and beyond the call of duty to get her what you think is the care she needs." Reid whistled quietly. "I'd say that's pretty admirable in an uncomfortable situation."

"It is uncomfortable. The authorities brought her to me…well, I'm not really sure how that worked out because once I realized they intended to leave her with me the rest of it turned into a blur. But there were some papers in the car—it was a car crash that killed them—and my name was on the papers. Papers from before we were divorced, I think.

"Anyway, the child was fine, so they brought her to me because they believed she was mine. Then they more or less coerced me into keeping her because they didn't have a place to put her for various reasons, she got sick, here I am…"

Reid laid a steadying hand on her arm. "And here you are, frantic."

"I'm sorry. In surgery I'm in control. But with Megan?" She shrugged. "It's hard, Reid. And I really don't have the right to be burdening you with all this. I wouldn't have, except she got sick and…"

"And you fixated on me as your solution."

"Not my solution. Megan's solution. You're her doctor. Which is a lame reason for me showing up here the way I did, but I panicked because my alternative was to take her to the hospital, and as a place to work it's fine, but for a child…" She stopped explaining. "So, how are we going to deal with all these problems I've created for you?"

He chuckled. "Minor glitches."

"I wouldn't call them minor as it involves more than I

ever expected. I mean, tying up your infirmary, keeping you away from your daughters. And your…wife?"

"No wife. Never married. Adopted daughters. Long story."

"Well, whatever the case, I haven't made things easy for you here, so…"

"So, that donation you mentioned?"

She nodded. "Happy to do it."

"Money's always great, but I'm thinking about some clinic time while you're here. That way I can sneak off and see my girls."

"I'm all for you getting to spend time with your daughters, and I'll do anything I can to help make that happen. But seriously? You want me working with your kids after what I just told you?" It was probably the most uninspired thing he could have suggested.

"Think of them as future adults and you'll be just fine."

"Wouldn't it be better if I simply hired a temp to come help you? Two temps, three. However many you need?"

"But you're going to have to stay here with Megan anyway. Or were you thinking about leaving her here with me and vanishing into thin air?"

She smiled an especially guilty smile, because that thought *had* crossed her mind a time or two. "Not thin air. I'm too easy to track down."

"But she's a ward of the state, and you, apparently, have been given some sort of temporary custody. Which means you can't just walk away from her. At least, I wouldn't think so. And I don't think you'd do that anyway, otherwise you'd have taken her to the hospital in the first place and just left her there." He grinned. "Or left her on my doorstep when you had the chance."

"OK, I'll admit it. Leaving her here might have crossed my mind…"

He chuckled. "You're too transparent, Keera."

"And you're too perceptive, Reid. But I meant what I said about children. So if you still want me to work with your kids here, knowing what you know about me, I'll give you a couple of days as I'm the one who messed you up. You'll have the right to terminate my services, with no notice, though. Just thought I'd throw that in there for your protection."

"What happens if you discover you don't mind working with children? Or, better yet, even like it?"

"I'll return to my blessedly all-adult practice with the memories. But you're not converting me, Doctor. If that happens, I'll concede a slight change of heart after the ordeal is over, if I have to—which I don't expect I will have to do. But that's all you'll get from me."

"OK, then. Now that the ground rules are established…"

"What ground rules?"

"The ones where I'm going to work super-hard to change your mind and you're going to fight me off every step of the way." He smiled, mimicking a gauntlet sliding over his right arm. "You threw down the darned gauntlet, so don't blame me for picking it up and seeing what I can do with it."

She couldn't help it. She liked this pediatrician, in spite of his choice of medical specialties. Liked his humor, liked his rather frazzled look. In fact, while the prospect of children underfoot didn't exactly appeal to her, spending a few days with Reid underfoot suddenly seemed like a nice way to pass time that would have been time lost in books and sleep. He was cute.

"Fine, I'll do what I need to do. But I wouldn't be putting on that other gauntlet just yet." To honor the deal, she extended a hand to him then had to bite her lower lip to keep from gasping when he took it, as the smooth feel of his skin on hers ignited a spark that arced all the way up her arm.

"So, about that IV…" he said, rather reluctantly. "Let me run over to the dorm for a minute then I'll be right back. In the meantime, maybe you could check over supplies. I'll start the IV as you don't do kids and you could get everything ready."

Backing his way down the steps, he only turned round when he'd reached ground. Or maybe he lingered. In her mind, the uncertainty she saw there most certainly had to be over his routine gone horribly wrong, but she wished it could have been more. And while she wasn't open to a relationship of any lasting sort, a nice flirtation from time to time wasn't off her list. Except this man ran a camp for kids, and he had kids of his own—a reality that slammed her back to earth in a fraction of a breath as she went looking for IV supplies.

But a little while later, after his round of goodnights had been said to his daughters, and as she watched him skillfully master the insertion of an IV catheter into such a tiny vein, she was almost changing her mind again. No flirting allowed! Admire the man, admire his skill. Every bit of this was trouble and if she was smart, she'd turn round, go home and hire him some temps.

But she wasn't smart. Not about the kinds of things going through her mind, anyway.

"You don't spend much time away from them, do you?" Keera asked, catching Reid staring out the door at the cabin where the girls were sleeping. Megan was tucked in for the night, resting as comfortably as she could under the circumstances.

"Try not to. I mean, I work, have to take call when it's my turn. But I have fantastic friends who look after them at home, which makes life easier for me. And now, even when they're here at camp, in the dorm, I can visit them when I want."

"If you want to be free to go over there whenever, I can spend the night with Megan."

"That's not it. I know they're safe, and just a few hundred yards away. But I'm over-protective. Can't help it. Emmie had leukemia when I adopted them. She was a little over two and Allie was still a baby. Their mother..." He shrugged.

"I never really knew what happened. Apparently, she brought Allie into the world so her umbilical cord stem cells could be used in treating Emmie. They're only half-sisters, but the match was perfect. Their mother—her name was Maria—stayed around long enough to see that Emmie was responding to treatment, and then one day she didn't come to the hospital. I'd heard she'd come here seeking medical care for Emmie, and once she'd found it she'd gone home to Mexico, but I really don't know.

"Anyway, after that..." He shrugged. "Emmie improved, Allie was placed in foster-care for a while, but there was always a thought that if the stem-cell therapy failed, there was still potential for a bone-marrow transplant, with a sibling donor. So, Allie was brought back to the hospital to stay, and that's where I met the girls, actually. Allie wasn't sick but she was put on my service to care for."

"And you adopted them?"

"It became legal six months ago. But I've had them for nearly four years. Because they had to stay together, and because of Emmie's leukemia, they weren't considered highly adoptable. Then the restrictions for adopting parents were huge because of the medical considerations. One thing led to another and I took them. I don't regret it."

"And Emmie, is she in remission?"

"I like to think of it as full recovery because she's so healthy now. But, yes, she's in remission. We've got one more year left before we can celebrate her *recovery*."

"Lucky girls," Keera commented.

"Lucky me. They slowed me down, forced me to look at life differently. I was on a pretty self-destructive path, indulging in just about every unhealthy kind of lifestyle habit there was. Smoking, fast foods three times a day, little to no sleep, amphetamines when needed. But when you have kids, you have to be...better." He smiled. "Or else they'll beat you down to a bloody pulp and walk all over you.

"Anyway, we have some choices here. The camp doesn't wake up for several more hours so, like I said earlier, you can go find the guest cabin and take advantage of the time while I stay here. Or you can stay with Megan while I take advantage of the next few hours. Your choice."

"My choice would have to be the noble thing, wouldn't it?" she said as she headed back into the clinic. "So save whatever's left of the night, and I'll be fine in one of the infirmary beds. Besides, I think it would be better if I stay closer to her because if she wakes up there's a chance she'll remember me."

"No arguments here. So, there are clean scrubs in the supply closet. Feel free to use the kitchen in the back of the infirmary and help yourself to tea, coffee, anything you want. And if you need me..." He held up his cellphone. "Or lean out the window and shout. I sleep with my windows open, and I'm a light sleeper."

"Literally?" she said, grabbing a pair of scrubs from the closet then pulling the curtain around the bed next to Megan's to afford herself a little privacy while she changed.

"Dad training is good for a lot of things," he said.

Megan's response was to whimper then turn on her side. Keera's response to that was to sit down on the edge of the bed next to Megan, lay her hand gently to her cheek to feel for a temperature then go immediately for a cold compress.

Reid, on the other hand, stood back and watched. Then decided that for someone who didn't like children, and who claimed she didn't have a way with them, Keera had a way with them. A very nice way, when her guard wasn't up.

One o'clock, two o'clock, and now it was going on three and he hadn't gone to sleep yet. In fact, he wasn't even sleepy. Which was highly unusual, because most of the time he was worn out by the time his head hit the pillow. His head had hit the pillow at least twenty times in the past three hours, but hadn't stayed there. All because Dr. Keera Murphy, the avowed child-hater, was next door, and she was all he could think about. Pretty, with her coppery long hair and her green eyes. Feisty with her opinions. But compassionate, in spite of her blustery no-kids-allowed attitude.

He'd seen the way she'd held Megan, and protected her. He'd heard the way she comforted her. Nothing about that showed any kind of dislike for the little girl, so he wondered why the attempt at an outward persuasion against children when he didn't believe that was her inner feeling.

We all have our fears, he reminded himself, returning to the bedroom window for at least the tenth time to look over at the infirmary, to the single light shining inside it. *Fear.* Such an immense word. His biggest fears were for his daughters. Always. And specifically for Emmie's health. What were Keera's fears?

He wondered about that as he thought back over the years, back to a time when his own life had been fearless. Or, as some might describe it, stupid. Actually, as he might describe it now that he'd grown up. He'd been typically bachelor-selfish, making his various conquests along the way. Doing nothing so different from the majority of hotshot interns and residents. Bad life, bad attitude, all changed for the love of two little girls.

And out of that love had grown his fears. But he wouldn't trade what he had now for anything from his old life because even now, thinking about the way he'd been made him shudder.

Or was he shuddering because he could see the silhouette of Keera in the infirmary? She was awake, like he was, and standing at the window, too. Looking over at him perhaps?

CHAPTER THREE

"I'VE GOT YOU set up in the guest cottage," Reid said, giving Keera a gentle nudge.

Keera opened her eyes, looked up and there he was, looking down at her, almost as disheveled as she felt. "What time is it?" she mumbled, rubbing her eyes, trying to focus, and hating the fact that the sun was already up to remind her she'd only gone to sleep a little while ago.

"Going on to eight. Did you sleep well?"

"Like a baby. For three hours. Megan had a restless night. She kept waking up, calling for her mommy." She glanced over at the child, who'd finally gone to sleep after several fussy intervals. "And she was spiking a pretty high fever for a while, which finally broke around four. Poor thing was miserable."

"Well, there's a nice shower waiting for you in the guest cabin, if that'll make you feel any better."

"If there's a bed in the shower, that'll be perfect."

"I don't know about you, but I used to have nights when three hours of sleep were a blessing."

"Back in my residency," she said, sitting up and stretching. "Which, thankfully, has been over with for a while. And my hospital had a very strict policy with its surgical residents about taking care of ourselves. If we came in and looked the least bit tired or sluggish, we'd get bumped out of the OR and they'd put us on chart duty and paper-work for the entire shift. Once or twice doing that and you learned to get your sleep."

"You were lucky, then. Where I did my Pediatrics res-idency, they were so short-staffed we were always tired and sluggish." He smiled. "Makes for a better story than well rested and perky, doesn't it?"

Keera laughed. "Want to hear about all the paper cuts I got the first time I had to spend a day on chart duty?"

"Good try," he said, holding out his hand to pull her out of bed. "But I can top that with the time I worked thirty-six hours straight in the middle of a blizzard, and I was the only pediatrician in the hospital. Didn't even get a nap in."

She swung her legs over the edge of the bed, then stood, and immediately brushed her hair back from her face. "Yes, but did you get physically wounded, the way I did? Paper cuts can get infected, you know."

"Do leg cramps, aching feet and a sore back count?"

"*Six* paper cuts, Reid."

"And the only food available the whole time was from a vending machine." He smiled. "Can't top that, can you?"

"Yuck. Vending machines? Seriously?"

"Nothing but snack cakes and candy bars and potato chips for thirty-six hours."

"Enough!" she said, holding out her hand to stop him. "You win. I can't top that because we had a catering ser-vice…even though I was barely able to hold a fork to eat my shrimp Louie salad."

"You just don't give up, do you?" he asked, leading her to the tiny kitchen in the rear where a fresh pot of coffee was awaiting her.

"Where I come from, giving up came with serious side effects," she said, pouring a cup for Reid first then one for herself.

"And where would that be?" he asked lightly.

"The streets," she said, quite surprised how that had slipped out so easily. Normally that was a piece of her life she didn't put out there for other people to know about. Too often they judged or pitied her. Gave her funny looks or were wary. None of which she wanted. "Growing up was rough. My mother and I had a hard time sometimes," she said, then took a sip. "I made it through, though, probably because I'm too stubborn to give up."

"Then I'd say stubborn suits you."

"Most of the time," she conceded. "Look, I need that shower you mentioned."

"Take all the time you need, as long as it's not longer than an hour. I've got clinic this morning after breakfast, and the kids will start lining up in about an hour. So I can watch Megan only until then."

"Clinic?"

"We do basic checks, vital signs, that sort of thing, just to make sure we're not wearing them out. Most of the kids are in early remission or recovery, and they're not always the best judges of how they feel, so we keep a pretty close eye on that."

"I could do that if you want to stay here for a while and rest, because you look about as strung out as I feel. And as that's my fault, the least I could do is some of your work."

"Sounds like an offer I shouldn't refuse," he said. "You take the clinic, and I'll stay here with Megan, get some paperwork done, do a supplies inventory, answer some long-overdue e-mails from parents interested in sending their kids to camp here."

"Do you have more than one session a year?"

"Actually, we run eight, various ages and stages of recovery."

"And you personally oversee them all?"

He shook his head. "I oversee the one Emmie attends. Which will probably change in another year or two when she'll be old enough she doesn't want Dad hanging around her all the time. For the other sessions I have some of the best medical help in the country come in." He smiled with pride. "People are generous."

"I'm impressed."

He shrugged off the compliment. "Kids need to be kids, no matter what their medical condition. Camp Hope simply facilitates that."

"And you're too modest."

"Not modest. Just grateful something like this worked out in my life. Like I told you, I was a real screw-up before the girls."

"Then good for the girls for bringing out all the potential in you. Anyway, let me go grab a quick shower then... what, exactly, will I do in clinic?"

"Vitals, a few meds."

"Anybody on chemo?"

"No, we don't do chemo here. Our kids have, for the most part, already gone through that stage a time or two. Although giving chemo's an option for the future because even kids who are that sick need a diversion, which Camp Hope would give them. Right now we just don't have the facilities for it. Someday, though...maybe a chemotherapy facility. Who knows, maybe even an entire hospital devoted to leukemia.

"Anyway, right now we do follow-up therapy with drugs for nausea, and a couple of our kids are getting prednisone and methotrexate. It's all basic stuff, pretty much. Each kid has a chart. Medicines are stored away according to the child." He handed her the key to the medicine storage. "So check their ID with the chart and, well...you'll figure it out.

"Betsy can come in later and help after her morning sickness has ended for the day. Just let me know if you need her, and I'll give her a shout."

"Basic stuff," she repeated. "I guess I find it difficult to believe you'd leave me alone with your kids. You don't even know me."

"The Internet's an amazing tool. I know what I need to know. As in do you want me to tell you what color dress you wore when you received your Surgeon of Distinction award last year?"

"I don't like awards and accolades."

"So you said in your acceptance speech. Oh, and it was black—with sequins. Nice look."

"Yeah, well, I prefer scrubs." With that, she turned away and headed for the door. Keera stopped by Megan's bed on the way out though and straightened her blanket. "I'll be back in a little while," she whispered. But the child didn't so much as stir, so Keera tiptoed away.

"Good morning, Doc Keera," the first boy said, as he held up his banded arm for her to read his name.

"Good morning." She looked at the band and smiled. "Gregory Carson. So, you get…" She glanced through his chart to see what was ordered for him.

He gave her a quizzical look. "Weight, temperature, blood pressure, pulse," he said. "And a pill for my nausea. It's what we all get, except the pill. I still need it. Some of the other kids don't."

"Really?" Gregory was astute. Very much on top of his condition. Which impressed her more than she'd been expected to be impressed.

He nodded. "Every day while we're here. Then I go to the doctor once a week when I'm home. Sometimes twice, if I'm not feeling well. I'm in early recovery, so they need to make sure nothing is changing."

The child was so matter-of-fact about his condition and, more than that, his whole life situation, that she wasn't even sure how to respond. "How old are you?" she asked him.

"Seven and a half, but you can consider me eight, if you want to." His broad grin revealed a missing tooth.

"Well, since you're *eight*, I think you're old enough to take some responsibility for yourself, like recording your own pulse, maybe taking your own temperature, and weighing yourself. The more control you take over your physical condition, the better off you'll be." Her check of him revealed his blood pressure, temperature and pulse to be normal. Weight consistent with the past several days. A little under his normal but not losing.

"Does that make sense to you?" she asked, as she recorded the numbers in his chart.

"I—I don't know. Isn't that what a doctor's supposed to do?"

"Or a nurse. Or your parents." She looked up from the chart and smiled at him. "Or, you, if you think you're old enough. I mean, almost eight…that's getting pretty old, you know."

OK, so maybe her doctoring approach was a little beyond his years, but it made sense that gaining more confidence in dealing with his condition would serve him well in the long run. Living with the idea that his cancer might recur had to be frightening, but spending every moment of his life depending on someone else to tell him he was doing fine had to be difficult.

Of course, she'd never had leukemia, never been chronically ill, but she'd spent too many years being dependent on someone else's conclusions about her, and it was such a helpless feeling.

"So, here's what we're going to do as soon as I can get it squared away on the schedule—and only if you think you're old enough to take on some responsibility. I want you to come back over here to the clinic, and we're going to talk about making your own choices. Then, if we have time, maybe I can show you how to do some medical procedures. But only if you want to."

He frowned, not sure what to say.

"Do you want to do that?" she asked him.

"Yes, I think so," he said, sounding nearly as tentative as she felt taking the initiative. But it was a good idea. She knew it! Would have loved someone teaching her the right initiatives to take when she had been as young as Gregory.

"Good. So, do you have a computer with you?"

He nodded. "It's mostly for games."

"Games, and in a little while we're going to start using it to track what doctors call your vital statistics. Do you know what those are?"

This time Gregory shrugged.

"Don't worry," Keera said, patting him on the shoulder. "It's easy stuff. But it's also very important. So, about your pill…"

After she shooed Gregory out the door, she went through much the same process with the next child, Charlie. Aged seven. And Heather, aged eight.

"So what are you teaching these kids?" she asked Reid an hour later, after all the kids, including Emmie, had gone through their routine morning check-up, and those who needed medication were medicated.

"Yesterday we went over some of the physiology of leukemia. Talked about white blood cells and how they—"

"They're not much more than babies, Reid. They don't

need the physiology lectures. What they need are the practical, day-to-day aspects of coping with their condition. They're all in some form of remission or recovery or whatever you want to call it, but they need to know what's normal for where they are in their recovery, and how to take care of some of their basic medical needs. Which I told a few of the older kids I'd teach them, if that's OK with you?

"And while I know you're so close to it, with your daughter in recovery, I think your tendency may be to baby them or protect them more than they should be protected."

"So you're here for one day and you know what's best for them?" It was said not so much in anger as in practiced reserve against the way he might really feel.

"That's not fair. I'm responding to a medical condition, and—"

"And you don't have a clue, Keera. Not a damn clue." Now the anger was peeking through, but only a little. "Last night you were pretty clear about how you don't like kids and now you're changing my program?"

"Not changing it. Just giving some of the kids a different option. You know, more control."

Reid took a deep breath to steady himself, then physically squared his shoulders. "OK, I know you want to help and I appreciate that, but these kids...they put all their trust in us, rely on us, and if you get yourself involved more than I asked you to, somewhere down the line one of these kids is going to put trust in you that won't be fulfilled.

"You can't do that to them, Keera. Medical procedures are one thing, but what you want to do is embark on a course that will change their lives in some way, and while I'm all for that, and would do it myself if I had time, the program this camp follows isn't about giving a few minutes of commitment then moving on. These kids depend on us, and you're about to step into the position of having them depend on you. Which isn't what you want, is it?"

He was right. She'd overstepped without thinking it through. She saw that now, and felt bad, especially as she was the intruder here. But her approach to medicine had never been laid-back. In fact, her approach to life had never been laid-back, and that's all Reid seemed to be—laid-back. Truthfully, her preference in men had always been for someone who was forceful. Of course, look what that had gotten her. Married to a man who had forced himself right out of their marriage and away with his mistress. Still…

"I didn't mean to do something I wasn't supposed to," she said. "And you're right. I don't want these kids relying on me then maybe getting hurt in the process. That's not what I meant to do."

"I know it's not. And to be honest, I'd love to expand my program here. But I don't have the means or the volunteers. Until we're larger, and can support larger programs, we're minimalists, and that's the best we can do."

"Then say the word and I'll tell the kids there's been a change of plans." She drew in a stiff breath as the sinking feeling set in that she was about to bite off way more than she'd ever expected to chew. "But I'd still like to do this, if that's OK with you. Because it is the right thing. Also because I promised and I don't want to let these kids down. So to prove how strongly I believe that empowering them over their conditions is the right thing to do, I'll…" Keera swallowed hard. "I'll stay for the week to follow through with teaching them. Only if you want me to, though."

"*Seriously?* You'd really stay and help?"

"Seriously," she said. Then instantly felt queasy.

"When I called you outspoken and opinionated, I guess I didn't know how much. But go ahead. You promised, and if the kids are expecting it, then we should give them what they're expecting." He grinned. Extended a hand to her. "Welcome to the staff of Camp Hope."

Or, in her case, Camp Hopeless, she thought as she shook his hand. "So, this is how I'm going to spend my summer vacation." Keera watched Reid's face, couldn't determine what he was feeling. He had an odd expression, and she didn't know him well enough to read it, but she could only guess that he was wishing she'd never come here. "It's the right thing, Reid. I promise, they're old enough."

"As interpreted by the doctor who doesn't like children?" he asked.

"As interpreted by the doctor who was forced to grow up too young and take on responsibilities no child should ever have to face. But it got me through. My independence is what saved my life many times over. And while you might not agree with me, I sincerely believe that giving these kids a bit of independence over their situations will save their lives, too.

"Maybe not in dramatic ways. Or maybe it will be in a dramatic way for one of them. Who knows? But, whatever the case, it's going to count for something. And, yes, it's also being interpreted by the doctor who warned you she wasn't good with children. I am good with my patients, though. Damned good, Reid, because I learned my childhood lessons well."

"And never had time to be a child?" he asked, his voice now sympathetic.

"I didn't need to be a child." With that, she moved past him into the infirmary to spend the next shift sitting with Megan and planning her first lesson—*"Taking your temperature."*

Poor Megan looked miserable, lying there in bed, with

a rash finally popping out on her. She was awake, though. Looking around. Alert. "Remember me?" Keera asked, keeping a sideways glance on Reid, who was trying very hard to seem busy with a supply inventory when she knew he was really trying to keep an eye on her. She didn't blame him. All things considered, she'd be doing the same if the situation were reversed.

Megan shook her head. "Want my mommy," she whimpered.

Keera didn't know how to respond to that so, instead, she said, "You came to visit me yesterday. Then I took you to play at the hospital, and we came here last night when you weren't feeling so well. My name is Keera. I was a friend of your daddy's."

"She was in a hospital daycare center?" Reid asked from across the room. "Exposing all the other children? Have you notified them yet?"

"You really want to be critical of me, don't you?" she said, smiling for Megan's sake, even though she was gritting her teeth underneath.

"You get high praise for surgery, but this isn't surgery, and I haven't seen enough of your style to know whether or not I'm a fan. But I'm giving you the benefit of the doubt here. You're out of your element, so that does start you off with a few extra points in your favor, since you're trying."

"Well, in or out of my element, I did call the hospital first thing this morning. Talked to the daycare director, let her know. Offered all the apologies I could muster. Unlike you, she wasn't grumpy about it. She said contagion happens all the time with kids and they simply look at it as a way to bolster young immune systems."

"You say that with a lot of indifference."

"No. I said it with a sigh of relief because I really don't like going around spreading infectious conditions everywhere I go. Especially here, where these kids have compromised immunity. But as far as the center goes, I got lucky because the director told me the children are all vaccinated before they're allowed in, that they sanitize the entire area several times a day, so not to worry."

She frowned. "Are you OK, Reid? Yesterday you weren't this…testy. In fact, you weren't even this testy earlier this morning. Is it because I suggested a program?"

"No. I'm just not a big fan of change."

"But I thought that's what you wanted for Camp Hope. Growth. Change."

"It is, but I don't have to adjust to it easily. That's just me. Kicking at progression when I'm the one egging it on."

"We do get used to our ruts, don't we?"

"Sometimes a rut isn't such a bad place to be. When Emmie was sick, she'd have these periods where she wasn't as bad, maybe not even sick at all, and I found myself praying to stay there. I didn't want to move forward, or sideways or backwards, for that matter. That one spot was…"

"Safe?" she asked.

He nodded. "Even though there was always the possibility that tomorrow might be even better, if today wasn't so bad, I didn't want to move away from it."

"Uncertainty can be paralyzing. When I was a child, nothing ever stayed the same in my life, and I think I was like you. If it worked, I didn't want it to change. But life changes every time we blink our eyes, doesn't it? And for Camp Hope, I was that blink."

"You're welcome here, Keera. I'm sorry your little girl is sick, but we'll manage it. It all just disrupted my routine, which…"

"Makes you grumpy."

He smiled. "Welcome to my world."

"We all have our quirks. You're likely to see my grumpiest come out if my surgical instruments aren't lined up a certain way on the tray. Or the wrong music gets played. I have a sequence I follow, never vary it, and if someone changes that, for any reason…" She shrugged. "Let's just say it can get ugly. I'm not mean, mind you, but I'm very demanding."

"I can't picture you any other way. Look, I'm sorry, Keera. Sorry I came at you so abruptly this morning, and I'm mostly sorry about my reaction to what's really a good idea. Because you're right, these kids do have to take responsibility for themselves, but sometimes when I look at them, all I see is…"

"Emmie. Who's spent most of her life being dependent on her daddy. I do understand that, Reid. For me it's a practical matter, and for you it's personal."

"What's personal is she doesn't need me so much any more. Which scares me, because at the end of the day I'm a father before I'm anything else. And it has nothing to do with her leukemia and everything to do with it. Maybe it's also because I don't know what normal's supposed to be. The three of us really don't have that in our family."

"Is being a single dad that difficult?"

"Yes and no. Because there's never been a mommy in the picture, we make it work the way it needs to. As they say, it is what it is. But I'd be lying if I told you that doing this alone is easy, because it's not. When the adoption became final, the judge congratulated me and told me single parenting is the new normal. Not sure what that's supposed to be, though."

"One person's lack of normality is another person's normality." Keera smiled sympathetically at Reid. "And as far as Emmie goes, she's seven. Trust me, what she's going to need from you has only just begun. And that has nothing to do with her medical condition." She turned her attention back to Megan, who'd dozed off again. "But what she's going to need…"

Her voice trailed off because Keera knew. Dear God, she knew in all the ways no child should ever have to know. Love was the start of it, which Reid had in abundance. And protection. And guidance. None of which she'd ever had given to her.

But Emmie, Allie and Megan would all need room to grow and develop as well, and that was something she'd created for herself because no one else had ever been there to help her. It was something Reid would eventually have to create for his daughters, like it or not, in spite of Emmie's physical condition. And something someone would have to create for Megan.

"Do you suppose if I wandered over to the dining hall, I might be able to beg a scrap of toast or a sandwich? Seems I haven't eaten since…" She thought for a moment. "Lunch yesterday. Except for an apple on my way here last night."

"That's an option. Or there's my kitchen. I wield a pretty mean toaster. And I have jam…"

"Please say strawberry!"

"Allie's favorite. Can't be without it."

"Then, by all means, lead me to Allie's favorite. I need a little fortifying before my first group of kids expect me to teach them the intricacies of taking a temperature. And maybe a couple of scrambled eggs, if you've got them."

"With green peppers and onions?"

"In my fondest dreams!" She smiled. "Oh, and, Reid? Don't worry. As fussy as you are over your daughters, I'm sure your girls will keep you in first place until they meet the boys who will steal their hearts away from you."

"Like I really wanted to hear that," he said, on his way out the door to go and fix Keera's meal.

Fifteen minutes later he returned with a tray complete with eggs, toast, and orange juice. Keera couldn't remember when something had smelled so good. Something about being at camp made her ravenous, and this was a perfect brunch. "You hungry?" she asked Megan, wondering if the child might eat a piece of toast.

Megan shook her head.

"Would you eat a small piece with strawberry jam on it?"

Apparently the bribe of strawberry jam caught her attention, because Megan nodded tentatively, then proceeded to eat an entire half a slice of toast and drink a small glass of apple juice before she slid back down into bed and rolled over on her side.

"You're persuasive," Reid commented.

"Strawberry jam is persuasive. I'm merely the means to that jam." She pulled the blanket back up over Megan and returned to finish her own food.

"So, how did your father manage it when you started to not need him as much?"

"He didn't," she said without a hint of emotion. "In fact, I was the daughter of a single mother. No daddy in my life. Not even in absentia. My mother…she wasn't interested in lasting relationships, I suppose you could say. Men came and went, none ever stayed."

She glanced at her watch. "I promised to squeeze my class in between agility training and lunch, if you could stay here with Megan for about thirty minutes. Or maybe one of the volunteers…"

"Sally Newton said she'd be glad to sit with Megan when we need her. She's a retired schoolteacher, loves the kids with a passion. Had leukemia herself when she was a child. So let me give her a call as I need to go and oversee agility."

"Am I making you late?"

"That's fine. It takes about ten minutes to get the kids settled down anyway, so I'll be just on time." He was finally feeling less stressed than he had all morning. Basically, he liked Keera. Liked her strength. Or, as some might call it, her brute force. And she was a force to be reckoned with, make no mistake about it.

He did have to admit, though, that he wasn't sure about her ideas about the children. On the surface it sounded good, and what she wanted to do with the children seemed reasonable, because he was all for these kids taking responsibility for various aspects of their health, even at their young ages. Keera seemed to have an agenda, though. She'd alluded to a rough childhood and needing her independence to get through it.

Still, there was something bigger. Something deeper. Maybe something to prove? And that's what worried him a little because the only agenda here was giving these kids everything they needed to be a kid in recovery. Simple plan with a single purpose.

He wasn't going to stop her, though, because he did see the value in it. And maybe when he got to know her better, he'd be a little more trusting. *Provided* he got to know her better. Which he hoped he would.

"Well, Dr. Reid, for a pediatrician you're a pretty darned good cook. My full stomach thanks you for the wonderful breakfast, or lunch, or whatever it was."

"My culinary skills thank you for the compliment. And just so you'll know, I can make a pretty good grilled cheese sandwich, if you're hungry later on."

"Good to know, just in case. Anyway, let me go sit with Megan for another ten minutes, then if you could ask Sally to come round?"

He nodded on his way out the door, stopping first at the sink to scrub his hands.

"And, Reid, the class is the right thing. I'm glad you're going to let me try it. I know you're worried, but I really believe these kids should take part in their care, and I want to get started because there's so much to teach them and I've only got a few days."

"I'd be lying if I didn't say I was concerned, because I am. Yes, it's important to empower them, but it could also be said that because their lives are so overwhelmed with their conditions they don't need to do anything more than they already do. You know, give them time to be children."

"How about giving them time to be responsible children? Because they do have to go about their lives differently, and you can't deny that. That's not robbing them of their childhood, though. It's only adding another layer to it."

"You don't ever give in, do you?"

She smiled. "Not unless I'm backed into a corner."

"No corner here. Although I'm going to warn you that for a woman who doesn't like kids, you're waging a mighty tough battle on behalf of these kids. Could it be the facade is cracking a little?"

"I don't have to like kids to want to do the right thing by them."

"You're right, you don't. But battles are waged because of passions, and you're waging a battle for them, Keera. Seems like someone's trying to fool someone, doesn't it?" He gave her a wink then grabbed a paper towel to dry his hands. "Now, let me go find Sally."

"Is her little girl sick like Emmie used to be?" Allie asked. She was sitting on the step outside when Reid left the infirmary.

"Aren't you supposed to be in arts and crafts?"

Allie rolled big, sad eyes up at him. A gesture that always melted him right down to nothing. Even at five, she knew that. "I missed you."

"And I missed you too, Miss Allejandra Lourdes Reid. But you need to go back to arts and crafts." He scooped the child up into his arms and walked across the compound with her, heading to the building where Allie should be occupied with finger-painting and sculpting with modeling clay, while the older children were involved in basic agility exercises on the obstacle course. "And, no, Dr. Murphy's little girl isn't sick the way Emmie was. Do you remember what I told you about something being contagious? How when some people get sick, other people can get sick from being too close to them? What Emmie had wouldn't make anybody else sick, but what Megan has can make people get sick if they get too close to her, which is why you can't go inside the infirmary. I don't want you getting sick."

"Will you get sick, Daddy?"

"No." And this was where he didn't want to launch into the explanation of vaccinations and how some illnesses, like measles, you'd only catch once. Which he'd had. "Doctors have special ways to protect themselves."

"Good," she said earnestly. "Because I don't know how to take care of you yet."

"Yes, you do," he whispered, as he headed down the back steps and handed the child over to Ciera, the arts and crafts volunteer. Hated like hell watching Ciera take Allie away.

Turning away to head off to agility training, he saw Keera watching him from the infirmary window, and wondered why someone like her didn't like children. What had she missed out on in her life that had scared her off so badly from what he believed to be one of the fundamental joys of life?

"You just don't know you like them," he said to himself. "But you will. Another few days here, and you will."

CHAPTER FOUR

"How did it go?" Reid asked, catching up to Keera, who was crossing the compound, her arms loaded with supplies, on her way back to the infirmary.

"Pretty good. We learned all about thermometers, what a body's temperature indicates, and how to take and read temperatures. I had them taking each other's temps, and I think there may be a few budding doctors in the group. Including Emmie. She's quite a little leader."

"As in bossy?" he asked.

"As in taking charge and being helpful. She's a sweet little girl, Reid. You're doing a good job with her. Oh, and she and Allie and I have a date for lunch in a little while. They want to show me something. Sally said she'd sit with Megan, so I hope that's OK? Because I asked the cook to pack us a little picnic. You're invited too. Something about the wading place."

He smiled. "The water's nice there. Not very deep. And so clear you can see the bottom."

"Well, apparently I need to go wading, and as I've never been, I've got able volunteers who want to teach me. All with your permission, of course."

"Something about being around a strong woman seems to be bringing out the best in my girls."

"I'm not overstepping the mark, am I?"

He shook his head. "They asked me first. I said yes."

"And you're coming?"

"I'll try. I need to do a physical on one of the kids, but that shouldn't take too long."

"Something wrong?" she asked.

He shook his head. "Physician request. It happens all the time."

"Good, then I'll see you at the wading place. But be warned, we might be talking *girl* things most of the time."

"See, that's the part of single parenting that's tough. They need a woman's touch, and it's just not there. I don't have a sister near by, and my mother and dad are in South America right now, running a medical clinic in Ecuador. No aunts or female cousins either."

"No girlfriend?"

"Had a fiancée for a while, but she didn't like the idea that I adopted a sick child. She thought it would take too much time away from her. And she was correct about that. It did. So she was right to dump me. Haven't really had time for a social life since then."

"Which leaves two little girls without a female influence in their lives."

"Right. It's amazing what you can pick up in the parenting magazines, though," he said, grinning. "I've got a whole stack of them, if you'd ever care to…"

She shook her head. "I was talking to social services a while ago, and they're going to place Megan with a nice foster-family as soon as she's medically able. And don't even begin to think I can be as generous as you and take her in, because I can't.

"She's the…well, she's not the reason my marriage ended, but she was one of the factors. My husband's secret baby. So while I know it's not her fault what her daddy did, and I totally understand that she's the only true innocent in a very ugly situation, I can't spend the rest of my life looking at her, knowing that…"

"That you failed?"

"Yes, I failed. But that's not even it. I didn't even know how to try. And Megan's that reminder."

"So you'll let her go to some stranger because of something you perceive as a lack in yourself."

"Fostering that little girl has never been an option for me. My lifestyle won't allow it."

"Yet you'll go on a lunch date with my little girls. That seems to conflict with your *no-kids-allowed* rule."

Stepping into the infirmary, Keera dropped her armload of supplies on the nearest desk, then spun to face Reid. "You did a good thing adopting your girls. You're a good man. A generous man. A very caring man. And that's all you.

"But I don't want the responsibility, OK? I feel sorry for Megan. My heart is breaking for her and I want to make sure she gets into a good situation. But that's not me. I work. I sleep. Then I work some more. Nothing there's going to change because I don't want it to change.

"So don't think that because I've agreed to give you one week of service here, and go on a picnic with your girls, that I'm going to come out of it with some big change of heart. My life is fine the way it is. It's not empty. I'm happy."

"And pretty damn defensive about it, too," he added.

"And pretty damn honest about it, Reid. I know what I can and can't have, and what you have…" She shook her head. "I can't have that."

"But can you have dinner? Tonight, after the kiddies are asleep? I've got enough people on call to cover us, I'm sure Sally will be fine spending an extra couple of hours looking after Megan, and there's an amazingly elegant little café about ten miles down the road. It sits on top of a mountain, and they say the sunset is breathtaking."

"In scrubs?" she asked. "Because that's all I have to wear."

"There's a little mercantile on the way. We could stop and do some shopping. Maybe for Megan as well, because she'll be up and out of bed by tomorrow or the day after."

An evening out with a man sounded surprisingly good. So did shopping for Megan. And while she and Reid didn't see eye to eye on a lot of things, she really liked him. Was curious to see him away from his element. "This isn't you asking me out on a date so you can get some personal satisfaction that you broke down my code a little, is it?"

He laughed. "Are you always so ungracious about what's just a simple gesture of friendship?"

"Not ungracious." She tilted her head up to look him straight in the eyes. "Just cautious."

"I don't want anything from you, Keera, except the days you promised me. Because, believe it or not, I'm as *cautious* as you are. Maybe even more, since I've got my daughters to consider."

"Then I suppose it's a date." She smiled. "Cautiously speaking."

"Eat one more bite," Keera encouraged Megan. Who would have guessed one bowl of soup could have taken so long? But Megan was being stubborn, and Sally was standing ready to swoop in and take over as soon as Keera admitted defeat.

"Maybe she's not hungry," the older woman said. "It doesn't always do to force children to eat if they don't want to."

"She's going to get too weak," Keera protested. "And

it's just soup." She felt totally defeated, failing at such a simple task.

"But does she like the soup?" Sally asked.

It had never occurred to her that Megan would have food preferences. Which just went to prove, even more, that she wasn't the one to take care of this child. "Do you like the soup?" she asked Megan.

Megan shook her head, indicating an adamant no.

"Then is there anything you would like to eat?"

"Strawberries," she said. "Want strawberries."

"Which would be toast with strawberry jam." She looked at Sally. "It's what she had for breakfast."

"And it's what she'll have for lunch. Let me run over to the kitchen, and I'll fix some."

"Is that all you want?" Keera asked Megan.

This time Megan nodded in the affirmative.

"They do have their opinions, even at that age," Reid said on his way in, as Sally flew out the door. He pulled out a stethoscope and listened to Megan's chest. "Bet you like peanut butter, too, don't you?" he asked the child, once he pulled the earpieces from his ears.

"Yes," she said. "And bananas."

"Then we'll see if we can find you some peanut butter and bananas for dinner. OK?"

Megan nodded.

"See, it comes naturally to you," Keera said. "And I don't have a clue."

"Well, I have an advantage. Not only am I a father, I work with children every day of my life. Before I went to med school I didn't have a clue, but I've learned. And that's what it's about, Keera. Learning. Trial and error, in my opinion, is the best way to figure it out. Oh, and she's not as congested as she was last night. I think the medicine is working. And as she's eating, it's time to yank the

IV. You want me to get rid of that nasty old tube in your arm, Megan?"

"It itches," she said, nodding.

"Well, we don't want you itching."

Keera stood back and watched the natural interplay between Reid and Megan, and admired the way he was so at ease with the child. It was like he knew exactly what she wanted. In a way, she envied that as it was a rapport she didn't have with her own patients. If ever there was someone who'd been put on this earth to work with children…

"Try," he prompted Keera.

"Try what?"

"To find your way in. One little thing—that's all it will take."

"Except I don't have a clue what that one little thing is."

"There's no specific one little thing. Like I said, trial and error. Think about something children love. Something you loved when you were a child."

She thought for a moment then smiled. "Megan, after you eat your toast and strawberries, would you like…" she glanced over at Reid, then back at Megan "…ice cream?"

Megan's eyes lit up. "Yes," she squealed.

"Then ice cream it is," Keera confirmed, feeling the same sense of accomplishment she usually felt after a long, grueling surgery.

"And you think you don't have a way with kids," Reid said. "One bowl of ice cream is going to go a lot further than you thought. Just wait and see."

"One bowl of ice cream doesn't make me parenting material. And even with that, you had to prompt me."

He laughed. "When Emmie was younger, and on chemo, getting her to eat was maybe the hardest thing I had to do, other than standing around and feeling so helpless. Bribes were good, though. What worked as often as not was a good honest talk with her about the importance of taking a bite or two. Kids her age…even kids Megan's age…do understand, and sometimes we forget that because we're so busy trying to convince them in a child's logic. But they live in an adult world as well, and you have to keep that in mind."

The adult world she'd known as a child had been harsh, cruel. Unfair. "I think it's better to let them live in their childhood world as long as they can, because when the adult world takes over…" She shrugged, then turned to Megan. "I'm going to get your ice cream now. Vanilla or chocolate?"

"'Nilla," she said, then smiled for the first time since Keera had known her.

Beautiful little girl, beautiful smile. She did look like her daddy, though. Especially the depth she saw in Megan's eyes. Kevin had always had that depth, had always seen things so deeply. She thought about their marriage as she dashed to the kitchen to scoop up the ice cream. It had started so well, all the regular hopes and dreams and plans. Then had ended so badly she'd blotted out most of everything past the midway point.

How did something like that happen to two people? It scared her because while on one level she understood how they'd grown apart, on a much deeper level she didn't understand it at all. Which meant she was doomed to repeat her mistakes—the reason why she wasn't going to do that ever again.

"Where'd you go?" Reid asked her, when she returned with the ice cream, only to find Megan munching away quite happily on a piece of toast.

"What do you mean? I'm right here."

"I don't mean in the literal sense," he said. "There was this look in your eyes when you came back in."

"Ex-husband stuff. Megan looks like him."

"And that bothers you?"

"Not really. But I was wondering how a marriage could go as wrong as ours did. There was a time when we were good, but it didn't last very long. And from the point we started losing, there was no way to get any of it back."

"But did you try?"

"Honestly, I don't know. Wouldn't have mattered, because he was already so invested in his other life."

"But you still loved him?"

"I'd like to say yes, or even no. But I don't know if I ever did, at least in the way you're supposed to when you commit your life to someone." She glanced down at the ice cream, and smiled. "But now I have his little girl, and I'm sure she'd prefer her ice cream not melted. So…" She stepped around Reid but stopped. "I'm not an indecisive person, Reid. Most of the time I'm probably more forceful than most people you know. Which is what made the end of my marriage so bitter, because it turned out that's the trait he hated most in me."

"As they say, 'One man's mistake is another man's opportunity,' or something like that."

"Only if she wants to be another man's opportunity. But I don't." And she meant it. Some people were meant to be alone, and she was one of those people. Although there were times she wished that weren't the case. "See you in a little while at the wading place."

The wading place turned out to be a wide spot in the pristine stream that ran serenely through the property. Surrounded by trees and rhododendron bushes, it was very isolated, and so clear and perfect that the pebbles on the bottom glistened like diamonds in the sun. Before they were even settled into a picnic spot, the girls had their shoes off and were wading across the shining pebbles, the water only coming barely above their ankles.

"I think I was just an excuse to come here," Keera said to Reid, who meandered in a few minutes after she was settled on the blanket. "This is…beautiful. It's a shame Megan couldn't have come along, too."

"Another day," Reid said, dropping down beside her. "To be honest, this spot is one of the reasons I bought the whole camp. I was looking at three different places for sale—two were former camps that had closed, and one was an undeveloped piece of property. I'd known for a while this was something I had to do." He smiled as he began to remove his shoes. "It came to me in a dream one night. Inspired, I think, by a picnic I'd taken the girls on earlier that day. Emmie was pretty sick, but she'd really enjoyed her time outside, and I thought about all the other kids with leukemia who barely ever get to see the light of day.

"Then I remembered all the fun times I had as a kid when I'd gone to camp…one thing led to another and I literally had a dream about being a camp leader.

"It stayed with me, so after a while I started looking into what it would take to set up a camp. The answer was, pretty much everything I had. But money's replaceable, you know. Children aren't. So I started looking, took the girls along with me. And when we were walking over this property and stumbled on this spot…well, you see how the girls reacted. What could I do?"

"Other than buy it for them and go broke."

Reid smiled. "So I'm flat broke for a while. No big deal. I have a good medical practice, and I'll earn it all back, and then some, over time. The thing about the camp is this is where I really learned to not think in terms of material possessions so much as value or worth. It changed my whole outlook on life. Allowed me to give something to the girls that goes beyond what money can buy."

"Allows you to give that to other people's girls and boys as well. I like the way you're putting your medical skills to other less traditional applications. I'm basically a traditionalist. I need four walls and surgical instruments, and anything else throws me for a loop. But this is…well, in a sense I suppose you could call it a hospital, because it does tend to the needs of children who need tending."

"A hospital without walls," he said. "I like that. So, are you coming wading, too?"

"Are there things in the stream that can bite me?"

Rather than answering, Reid nearly doubled over laughing. "Maybe tadpoles," he finally managed, "but I don't know if they even have teeth."

"I'm serious. I've never really been a nature girl, and sometimes I'm not so brave in the unknown."

He pointed to his daughters, who were busy splashing each other.

"OK, I get it. If they aren't afraid, I shouldn't be afraid."

"And I won't desert you, Keera. If I see a menacing tadpole swimming in your direction, I'll shoo it away."

"My knight in shining armor," she said, as she slid out of her sandals and rolled up the bottoms of her scrub pants.

"It's hard to believe you've never been wading," he said, extending a hand to help her up off the ground. "Makes me wonder what other kinds of things you've never done that I might be able to show you."

She took his hand and let herself be pulled to her feet. But once she was up he didn't let go of her hand. Instead, he held it as they walked towards the stream. Like lovers, they strolled along the path, hand in hand, shoulder to shoulder, as if they'd done it before. Or should have done it before. "I've lived a sheltered life," she admitted at the stream's edge. "You know, die-hard city girl."

"Well, welcome to the country, city girl." He led her into the water. She clung to him even harder.

"It's not like a wading pool," she said as she relaxed.

"No, it's better."

"Yes," she almost purred. "It's much, much better." But she wasn't sure what, exactly, was better. Was it the water or the fact that she liked holding Reid's hand? Or the fact that he still wasn't letting go? That was the part she liked best, she decided. Definitely the part she liked best.

"It's only for a week," Reid said, laughing as Keera picked out the tenth outfit for Megan. Clothes, plus dolls, accessories, all kinds of little-girl things.

After a little wading and a quick picnic, they'd returned to camp and she'd spent the rest of the afternoon with Megan, reading to her, playing games, even watching her sleep. Something about the child pulled her in. Maybe it was the fear she saw in her eyes, or that look of being a little girl lost. A look she was sure she herself had had most of her childhood.

Her heart did go out to Megan, more and more with every passing minute, because each minute brought the poor child closer to the reality that awaited her. A reality Keera couldn't change. So even after an afternoon spent renouncing the material things in life, Keera was having a good time trying to compensate for Megan's terrible losses by piling new material things on it. And, admittedly, she loved little-girl shopping, and wished desperately Megan could have come along to be part of it.

"I want her to have nice things wherever she goes to. Wherever social services puts her."

"I imagine they'll gather up some of the things she already owns," he said.

"Which will only remind her of what she's lost. No, I'll buy her everything she needs for her new life."

"But what if she has a favorite doll or book? Doesn't she deserve to have those with her?" He liked this fierce attitude she was taking up on Megan's behalf. Whether or not she wanted to admit it, Keera was investing a little of herself in that child, and that was a good thing. Although Reid wasn't about to fool himself into believing that she would keep the child, as she'd been brutally honest about that more than once.

"What she deserves is to move into her new life without sadness left over from the old one," Keera said as she grabbed the cutest little pink, fuzzy pajamas off the shelf, looked them over, then went back for an additional pair in yellow.

"So, what about you? We've been here an hour, our reservations are in twenty minutes, and you're still in your scrubs. Remember how we came here to buy you something respectable to wear to dinner tonight?"

"Twenty minutes?" Keera rolled the shopping cart at Reid, then spun away. "Go ahead and start checking out," she called back to him as she literally ran to the ladies' department. "By the time they get most of it rung up…" The rest of her words were lost as she rounded a corner, while he stood in the middle of the aisle, simply smiling. Losing her had definitely been her ex-husband's mistake. Huge mistake!

It was a thought still on Reid's mind a few minutes later when Keera skidded into the checkout line behind him, her arms loaded with…well, he wasn't sure. Dresses, underwear, shoes? No way she could have done all that shopping in such a short time. But, as it turned out, she had, because as the last of Megan's items were scanned, Keera added her armload to the end of it. After she'd paid, she grabbed one of the bags and headed straight for the ladies' room, from which, a minute or two later, she emerged looking remarkably put together in her little black dress, matching shoes, and…make-up.

"How did you do all of that in…?" He glanced at his watch, exaggerating a shrug.

Laughing, Keera brushed her fingers through her hair. She'd pulled it out of its no-nonsense ponytail a minute earlier, but hadn't had time to run a brush through it, and it looked like the mane of a wild horse. Untamed, a bit flyaway. But she was dressed otherwise, and actually felt pretty good about the way she looked. "Years of practice, street clothes to scrubs in a minute flat. My best record." She grinned. "This took a little longer."

"Longer? I think if you could patent the formula, husbands all over the world would buy it. I know my dad and my brothers-in-law would."

"Just a matter of practice," she said, taking several of the bags from Reid then following him out to the car. "My mother and I had to…let's say we had to be on the move at any given second, so I learned early on that I either had to be fast or things got left behind." Including her, several times.

"Well, you look amazing," he said, eyeing her from head to toe. "Can't imagine how you'd improve on it if you'd had, say, half an hour."

"Primping for half an hour's a waste. In that same thirty minutes I could have a patient totally prepped for an incision. Or have that incision made, and be well on my way to exploring an occluded artery."

"Nice dinner conversation," he said, holding open the car door for her.

"Except we're not at dinner yet." Stepping in, she smoothed her dress and tried to pull it down a little over her legs, but it was a bit short, riding halfway between her knee and thigh when she stood and scooting up even shorter than that when she was seated. A fact she caught Reid checking out. Surprisingly, she liked seeing that he liked what he saw. "And I promise to be on my best behavior as soon as we arrive at the restaurant."

"Coming from you, that almost sounds boring."

"Maybe it will be," she said, as he climbed in next to her. "So, you're sure it's OK, both of us being away for the evening? And your girls?"

"Tonight I'm running second place to cook's basset hound, who's the dorm guest for the evening. Besides, I promised the girls I'd tuck them in later."

"Do you read them bedtime stories?"

"Sometimes. Or we just talk. They tell me about their day, I modify my day for them. We talk about their plans for the future. Those kinds of things."

"Sounds nice."

"Didn't you ever do that with your mother?"

"My mother was…she was usually working when I went to sleep. We didn't have a lot of time for the traditional mother-child kind of thing. Or, in your case, the daddy-daughter thing."

"Too bad, because I enjoy it. Probably more than my girls do. For them it's a bedtime ritual, but for me it's about staying in touch and keeping myself involved in their lives."

"Lucky little girls," she commented, settling in to watch the view.

All those years ago, when she'd moved to Tennessee, it had been to get away from the harsh realities her life had slammed her with. Being the daughter of a prostitute hadn't been easy. Neither was big city life when you were a little girl alone. So she'd promised herself someplace nice when she got away, and that was the first thing she'd done.

She'd loved Tennessee, loved the mountains, the blue skies. Even loved the occasional bear that had come raiding her trash cans at night. For Megan's sake, she hoped the child would have an adoptive family who stayed in Tennessee. A family like Reid's.

Or…would he adopt her? Would he want one more daughter to tuck in at night? Traditional families were good and social services usually held out for those, but untraditional or single-parent families were good, too. Just look at Reid's family. As a child, she'd have loved having a parent like him instead of what she'd had.

So, maybe seeing if Reid would adopt Megan would be worth pursuing. Just not now, though. She'd have to wait until he knew her better and got attached to her. She'd also have to wait until she knew if Reid even wanted more children. Although he certainly seemed like the type who would.

"But overall a situation like yours wouldn't do for me. Like I said, I'm not cut out for it. Half the time I'm not even home at bedtime, and if someone expected me to tuck them in or read to them, they'd be out of luck."

"You really don't want children, do you? I've known a lot of women who say they don't but they eventually change their minds. Especially when their biological clock…" He stopped, exchanged a quick glance with her. "None of my business, right?"

"I don't hide the fact, Reid. Never have. So it doesn't matter whose business it is, because it's simply a statement of fact. And even when my so-called biological clock starts ticking, nothing's going to change."

"Even if you meet the man of your dreams who wants children?"

"*Especially* if I meet the man of my dreams, because he's not going to want children. That's part of my dream."

"You're a hard case, Dr. Murphy. And you'll be quite a challenge for some man someday."

"I take that as a compliment, Dr. Adams." So maybe the harder she pushed the child away, the more he might be inclined to keep her. Because she truly wanted Megan to have a daddy like Reid. All children deserved to have a daddy like Reid.

"The mountain trout is wonderful," she said, taking the last bite of her food. "Everything about this restaurant is wonderful. Do you bring the girls here?"

"No, they prefer pizza. But every now and then I need some adult food, and an evening without the girls, so The Trout is usually my destination. An hour from Sugar Creek gives me a nice drive, time to relax. Nice scenery along the way. Then all the ambiance here."

"I guess I'm surprised you'd leave them."

"Sometimes you have to." He grinned. "Parents have lives too, you know. And Brax—my partner's father— loves taking the girls for pizza, along with his grandkids. They have a pizza night once a week."

"So, how does parenting work with your medical practice?"

"My partners, Deanna and Beau, have a couple of children, and Brax is always ready to babysit. So they were more than happy to throw my girls into the mix when I moved there. Like I said, there's pizza night, and Brax is always willing to stand in if I'm called out."

"Sounds like you got lucky."

"I did. We originally lived in Memphis—it's where I

did my residency, then I stayed. But that's where Emmie was so sick for so long, and I didn't want her to always have the reminders around her. So, when her medical care scaled back to where it is now, we started over. Little town, big life. It's perfect for us. And with the camp being so close..." He shrugged. "It works."

"So, have you ever considered adding a Mrs. Adams to your family? I know you said you're not dating right now, but what about the future?"

"She'd have to be awfully special. Like I said, I'm pretty protective of my girls, and I don't want to upset the balance only to find it doesn't work."

"Like my marriage. Definitely a balance out of whack there."

"But you got out before there were kids." He swallowed hard, looked embarrassed. "Well, except the one."

"Except the one," she repeated.

Keera was so easy to talk to. In fact, Reid had never known someone he'd wanted to open up to the way he did with her. Maybe it was because she was safe. Because she wasn't out to snag a doctor the way so many women in his past had been.

With his past couple of dates, the subject of marriage had come up almost immediately. Marriage, the future as a couple, building a house together...first-date nonsense in which he didn't want to indulge. Besides, if they'd known what they were trying to snag—a doctor whose every last cent went to his camp or to his daughter's medical care, who worked more hours than any one should ever have to, who lived in a rented, cramped cottage rather than owning a sprawling mansion—there wasn't much there to snag.

He chuckled to himself. It wasn't the lifestyle he'd thought he'd have when he'd committed to being a doctor. No, it was a much better one. He wouldn't trade a second of it, hard knocks and all.

"So, have you given any thought about what you're going to do with Megan once she's better? Keep her until social services place her, give her up right away?"

"Hope that social services can find her a good situation as soon as possible. Or maybe that's something I could do. She deserves someone who wants children. Someone who wants to be a mommy or a daddy, together or separately."

"Which is still not you?"

Keera laughed. "Which is *still* not me. Good try, though."

"She's an amazing little girl. Smart. Very pretty."

"And very much the product of an affair that was, in part, responsible for the demise of my marriage."

"Ah, yes. The illegitimate child."

Infuriated, Keera spun to face him. "Don't you dare call her that! Whatever her parents did isn't her fault and she shouldn't have to…" Stopping, she saw the amused look on his face. "OK, I get it. You're testing me. Trying to see if I might have feelings for her. Or if I would come to her defense. Well, yes and yes. I'm not heartless, Reid. I just know who I am."

"You're sure about that?"

She hunkered down into her chair and folded her arms stubbornly across her chest. "Absolutely. I've had a lot of years coming to terms with me, and I know exactly who I am and what I'm about."

Sometimes, though, she did wonder how much she really knew, or didn't know. After all, she was spending a week at a camp for kids, even enjoying it, and nowhere in her knowledge of herself would she have ever thought something like that could happen.

"Look, it wasn't my intention to turn this evening into

a battle. How about we get off the subject and talk about something else? Because the cherry cheesecake here is the best in the whole state, and I don't want you missing out because I've said something to get your gut roiling. So…" He tried coaxing her with a smile, and only succeeded in getting the scowl off her face.

"Maybe the weather? Or the fact that I'm backpedaling on my opinion of what kinds of responsibility I think the children at Camp Hope can handle?"

No luck moving back to neutral territory yet. He tried again. "Medical school? We could talk about that. Like what made you decide you wanted to be a doctor?" He watched, saw her face soften a bit. Let out a sigh of relief. "I'll start off by telling you mine then you can tell me yours."

"Mine isn't much to tell," she said, relaxing a little.

"Neither is mine. I came from a large family, three sisters, two brothers. I was the oldest, always in charge of looking after the younger ones. My parents are both doctors, by the way. Dad's a surgeon, Mom's an anesthesiologist. So I grew up in the life. As it turned out, they produced a family of doctors. I have a brother and two sisters still in med school, one brother in his surgical residency, and a sister who's a full-fledged obstetrician."

"Which means your parents were good role models," Keera commented.

"They were. Still are. But it was a hectic life growing up, never being able to plan anything when they were on call. Never being able to count on them coming to school events."

"Don't tell me. You played clarinet in the band."

"Almost. I was the quarterback on the high-school football team. It got me a scholarship to college, so I played in college, too."

"Sounds like a charmed life," she said.

Her face was so impassive he didn't know what to make of it. "Not charmed. We were like any other family, with our ups and downs."

"Which is why you know how to be a good father now. Because you understand all that."

"Some of it. Although I'll admit my girls present me with challenges I could never anticipate. The thing is, when I ask my mom for advice, she usually smiles and tells me to go with my instincts. Like that helps."

"But she's right. At the end of the day, all the parenting books in the world are only words when you have two little flesh-and-blood human beings to deal with. Children, I might add, who haven't read the parenting books and don't know the proper way you're supposed to be parenting them."

"Good insight for a non-parenting type."

Finally, she smiled. "I grew up poor. Good insight was about all I had to get me through."

"You mentioned that your mother worked a lot?"

"Sometimes days in a row."

"And no father, so what about brothers and sisters?"

She shook her head. "It was only the two of us."

"But you got to medical school. How did that happen?"

"Getting an education wasn't easy because we moved around a lot for my mother's work. Anyway, I liked knowledge, so when I wasn't able to go to school I'd find a library and read. Anything, everything.

"I really liked the sciences and found out, early on, that I loved biological sciences. From there it was reading about human anatomy, and the next logical jump was medical articles and textbooks. I practically memorized *Gray's Anatomy*, and by the time I was fourteen or fifteen there probably wasn't an advanced physiology book

I hadn't devoured. Knowledge was my...everything. And all that reading got me a college scholarship."

"I'll bet you passed your med-school exams without batting an eyelid."

"I did," she admitted. "I was told I was one of the top scorers in the country. And the rest, as they say, is history. I made it through, found my job, secured my future."

"And your mother. Is she proud?"

Keera shrugged as she picked up her coffee cup. "I haven't seen her since I was thirteen. The state took me away from her, put me in foster-care, except I was too old for most foster-homes. I went to a few, but they didn't work out so I spent the remainder of my formative years in the guardian home as a ward of the state."

This wasn't what he'd expected. Not at all. "I...I don't know what to say."

"There really is nothing to say. My mother was a prostitute, and by the time I was thirteen she was expecting the same from me. We lived in cardboard boxes in alleys and in the backseats of abandoned cars. Sometimes we'd find a vacant house, or rent a room where the roaches and bed bugs were thicker than the nicotine stains on the ceilings. Sometimes she'd be gone for days, and I'd have to scrounge for food in garbage cans.

"That was my life, Reid, until the authorities caught up to us and took me away. Something I don't talk about because it's in the past."

"I'm so, so sorry." Now he understood her need for independence. "But you've done an amazing thing. Most people—"

"Most people would have let it beat them down, but I didn't. It's no big deal. In fact, the only big deal I want to talk about now is that cheesecake. And if it's as good as you say, I want two pieces. One for now, one to share with Megan tomorrow."

For once he didn't know what to say, didn't know how to respond to her indifference. But maybe he didn't have to. Keera had given him insight into the strongest woman… no, make that the strongest person…he'd ever known. But she wanted to take cheesecake back to Megan, which meant that maybe he'd be able to help her find an even deeper insight into that same person—the softer side of her. Because whether or not she wanted to admit it, it was there.

And whether or not he wanted to admit this to himself, he thought he might be a little in love. Or at the very least head-over-heels infatuated. "Waiter, seven pieces of cherry cheesecake, please. Two for here, five to go." He glanced over at Keera, who once again wore her typical impassive expression. "One for you and me tomorrow when we give the girls their cheesecake."

"Cheesecake two days in a row. Sounds decadent."

"Decadent but good." He reached across the table and took her hand. "And for what it's worth, I like your strength. But you do have a gentler side, Keera. You just don't let it out."

"Because I don't want it to get out. Softer sides are what get you hurt."

"Or what make you human."

She shrugged. "Softer sides aren't all what they're cracked up to be. Personally, I like being tough around the edges and all the way through."

"But I see you, Keera Murphy. And I know better."

"Then quit looking so close, Reid, because if you think there's anything more there, you're only seeing what you want to see."

"Or what you want to project."

She pulled her hand from his. "What I want to project is who I am. You know, what you see is what you get."

"And what I see is someone who isn't comfortable with her softer, gentler side."

"What you're seeing is someone who doesn't have a softer, gentler side."

"Is that a challenge?" he asked, smiling

"It's a fact."

"We'll see," Reid warned, as the waiter placed the cheesecake on the table. "We'll just see." Truly, he was looking forward to what he would see.

CHAPTER FIVE

"Ok, you're looking at it upside down," Keera said. "Turn it over, take a look at the numbers, then tell me what you're seeing."

Gregory studied the digital thermometer for a moment, frowning at first as he pondered it, then finally smiled and pronounced, "Ninety-eight point six."

"Good! Now, tell me what that means." Megan was inside asleep, within earshot, and Keera was teaching today's class outside, on the infirmary's front steps. Her hospital without walls. Or, in this case, her classroom without walls. When she'd been homeless as a child, she'd loathed being outside. Now she couldn't get enough of it.

"It means perfect," Gregory said, smiling. "I don't have a fever."

"Excellent! So, what do you do next?"

"I write it down in my journal?"

"That's right. But how?" she asked him.

"I write the date first, then the time, then the temperature."

"Very good!" she exclaimed, actually feeling pride in his accomplishment. "I'm proud of you for learning so quickly. So now I think that tomorrow you'll be ready to move on to taking your pulse. Remember what I said about that? That it's the number of times your heart beats per minute."

"And normal is from sixty to one hundred. I read that on the Internet last night." Gregory beamed from ear to ear. "I texted my mom, told her I want to be a doctor like you and Doc Reid. Do you think I can do that, Doc Keera? Do you think I can be a doctor when I grow up?"

"I think you can be anything you want to be, Gregory. And if that's a doctor, you'll be a very good one."

He stood up from the chair he'd brought outside and crossed over to Keera, who was sitting on a step, and gave her a great big hug. "That's from my mom," he said when he backed away. "When she texted me back she said she was happy, and to give you a hug for her."

Surprisingly, Keera was touched by the simple gesture. She'd taught a little boy to take his temperature and it was like she'd taught him a valuable life skill that opened up a whole new world of possibilities for him. Who knew? Maybe it had.

Simple accomplishments and small steps to a child were life-changers, she suddenly realized. Too bad she hadn't had an adult in her life to show her how that was…*how anything* was when she'd been Gregory's age.

Somehow, fighting to survive took precedence over just about everything else because, back in the day, her small step had been a full belly and her simple accomplishment a place where she could take an honest-to-goodness bath. Of course, those life skills had taught her how to survive, hadn't they? And they'd made her as tough as nails. All in all, not bad skills to have in the life she lived now. At least, that's how she chose to look at it. But she was still very proud of Gregory.

"His mom called me a little while ago," she told Reid a couple of hours later. "She was actually crying, she was

so elated over a silly little thing like taking a temperature. It was…"

"Gratifying?" Reid asked her.

"I was going more for embarrassing. But I suppose it
was gratifying." She was sitting at the front work station
in the infirmary. Reid had made coffee and he'd poured
two cups for them. Megan was awake, sitting on the side
of the bed, playing dolls with Sally and intermittently
watching a video cartoon.

"When you wake up in the morning and don't know if
your child will survive the day, even the silly little things,
like taking a temperature, can make you grateful." Sitting
down across from her, he took a sip of his coffee. "I had
some pretty rough days one time when Emmie was having
a particularly bad crisis. She'd been on chemo for a while,
it was her second time, and she'd lost her hair. That, plus
she didn't have enough weight on her body to sustain her.
She was always so cold. Nothing made her warm up, and
she'd lie in bed, under the covers, and shiver so hard…"

He paused and swallowed hard, and Keera reached
across to lay a comforting hand on his arm. But said nothing, because her words would only intrude on a moment
that required nothing more from her than compassionate support.

Their eyes met for a moment, stayed locked on each
other until Reid finally broke the silence. "Do you know
how beautiful your eyes are?" he asked, totally out of the
blue.

"My eyes?" she asked, keeping her hand in place.

"Beautiful eyes. Like Emmie's are. But when she was
sick…the only way I can describe them is hollow," he continued after a moment. "They were hollow and so distant.
It was like my little girl was slipping away from me, Keera.
She was getting further and further away every time I

looked into her eyes, and there was nothing I could do to get her back. I think that was the first time I really, truly thought I m-might lose her." He pulled his arm away from her hand, and reached up and stroked her cheek.

"But I remember sitting there at her bedside one afternoon, watching her look out the window at a little bluebird that had landed on the ledge. It was looking in at her, and she laughed. Her eyes were bright again, so full of life just for that single moment—a moment that froze in time for me. And her laugh—I hadn't heard it in months, but when she laughed, well, I can't begin to describe how grateful I was to hear it. It gave me hope.

"For the first time in I don't know how long I finally let myself think about a future, about how things were going to get better for her. A simple laugh from Emmie or making plans to be a doctor from Gregory, it's the same thing. It's about hope.

"And for a kid like Gregory it's everything because he's never made plans for the future, like most kids do. You know, things like when I grow up I want to be a firefighter or an astronaut. This was the first time his mother has ever heard that from him, and it's because you gave him a different kind of hope for his life. With that one simple accomplishment. You showed him he can have a life."

"I don't know what to say," she murmured, quite touched. "In surgery I know I make a difference, like save a life, but it's never quite so…I guess the word is *profound*. They thank me, I wish them well, and it's all well and good. It's what I'm supposed to do because I'm good at what I do. But it doesn't affect me one way or the other."

"Because you won't let it affect you."

"Because I don't want it to affect me. If I were to get involved on the kind of personal level you seem to be involved with your kids on, I would lose objectivity. Become too vulnerable to things that could, ultimately, diminish my work as a surgeon. And I can't afford to lose that objectivity because, for me, that's what saves the lives of my patients."

"It's not your objectivity that saves lives, Keera. It's you. Who you are."

"Who I am is what I do, and I'm fine with where I am in that equation. You know, one equals the other. It's good. I'm used to it, and it works for me like your life works for you." She smiled as she gripped her cup. It was a sad, reflective smile, though. "But you really don't like the way I live my life, do you?"

"I'm not judging you, Keera. Please don't think I am. But I think the bigger question is: do you like the way you live your life? Because I'm not sure you do."

"What I like is the result I get at the end of the day when my surgeries are over with and my patients are stable."

"But isn't there some loneliness in that result? Because without my girls, no matter what I've done for my patients, that's all I'd have if Emmie and Allie weren't there to remind me that I have a purpose outside being a doctor."

"Being a doctor is my purpose, though. The only one I want. And the result I get doesn't come with loneliness. More like…well, to use your word, I experience gratification because I enjoy my work, and I also enjoy the ability to make things turn out the way they should."

"You're talking about results, though, not people. Do you ever see your work in terms of the people involved? Or having something more than work-related gratification? Maybe being happy? See, for me, being a pediatrician makes me happy. Sure, it's gratifying, but I want more than that. And being a pediatrician, working with kids the way I do, I find it."

"Isn't enjoyment the same as being happy, though?"

He shook his head. "I enjoy a good ice-cream cone, and maybe for the moment or two I'm eating it I feel a certain sense of happiness. But that's not the deep, abiding kind of happiness I want, or need, in my life."

She paused, thought about his question for a moment, then shook her head. "Then if I don't have the same kind of happiness in my life that you have in yours, does that make me shallow? Because in terms of my patients, good results do make me happy. I want all my patients to have a good result.

"But as personal involvements outside my professional life…if I did get involved personally then my objectivity would fly out the window, and I can't afford that in order to go after that elusive happiness you're talking about. People trust me for a certain outcome and it gets right back to how I'm gratified I can make that happen. Like it or not, that's who I am."

Reid reached across the table and laced his fingers through hers. "That's who you *think* you are. But there's more to you, Keera. There's a genuine quality I don't think you recognize, but I can see it and when you're ready to see it, you will."

"Or maybe I won't. You're the real deal, not me, and we can't all be you, Reid." She wanted to be offended by his comments and presumptions and especially by his intrusion, but there was nothing about Reid she could be offended by because she was right. He was the real deal. Genuine, caring. And she liked his touch, liked the way his friendly gestures toward her seemed so natural.

In fact, they seemed so natural she feared they could be become habit-forming. But she wasn't reading anything into them other than friendship because that's the kind of man he was—the kind who made friendly gestures, squeezed an arm, held a hand, without pretense or thought.

"You have a good life. Probably a great life. One most people would want. But that's not me, Reid. If anything, I'm probably the most self-aware person you've ever met, and the one thing I'm most aware of is me. I am who I am, and I accept that, even for the things you see as limitations. Or character flaws."

"Yet you must have had a romantic notion once, because you got married. And marriage is all about seeking happiness. You know, happily-ever-after."

As reality sank in and she realized how much she enjoyed his lingering touch, she unlaced her fingers from his and gripped her coffee cup with both hands.

"Happily-ever-after is a myth, and when I got married I was in love with the idea of being in love. It's everywhere you look, everywhere you go. You know, you have to be in love, or be nothing or no one. Television and movies revolve around it; the advertising world makes billions selling it. Mothers teach their daughters that to be fulfilled you have to grow up and marry a Prince Charming, and the bestselling books on the market are all about finding that one true love.

"So, yes, I bought into it for a little while, but I don't think I ever really loved him. Not in the traditional sense. If I had, I would have been more involved in our marriage, and fought harder to keep it." She shrugged. "But I wasn't involved, although he really should have divorced me rather than cheating. Because I believe in absolutes, and in a marriage that's one of them. If you do the deed, you do it the right way or you don't do it at all."

She pushed back from the table. "Look, I promised Megan we'd play some games, and right now Sally's having all the fun with her. It's my turn. And I was also thinking that now, as she's feeling better, maybe we could expand our horizons a little since she's not too happy about being confined. So, you're the pediatrician. How long before she can go outside?"

"Today, if she's up to it. But as the contagion period is four days before the rash and up to four days after, I still don't want her around the children. So if you could take her out somewhere east of the hospital—we don't have activities out there today, and it's a pretty area. I think she should enjoy it."

"Yes, if she's up to it. Or maybe we could sit out on the porch for a while. Whatever works best for her. And you? What's on your agenda for the rest of the day?"

"Nature hike down to the river, a picnic lunch, then some well-managed, very tame river-rafting. I have a company coming in this afternoon that specializes in river adventures, and the kids are going to have their first outing in a rubber raft. The gentle kind, not the white-water kind that goes over rocks and waterfalls."

"Sounds like fun. They're going to enjoy it. I know I would have when I was their age." She smiled. "You take very good care of these children, Reid. They're fortunate to have you."

He certainly knew how to make a difficult childhood bearable, and while her childhood couldn't compare to what all these kids had gone through, she wondered how she might have benefited from having someone like him in her life when she had been a child. Yes, these children, and especially his daughters, were very, very lucky.

"It's not just me. A lot of people are generous with the kids. Tomorrow we're going on a zip line. You know, when you harness up and zip across a wire from tree to tree?"

"The kids are all up to it?" she asked, genuinely surprised.

"It's the training facility. Very tame, very safe. And like the rafting, I think they'll love it because it's something they haven't been able to do before. Then in a couple of days my medical partner's coming in, bringing in a few of his horses for the kids to ride. Horseback riding is always a highlight around here and we try to get it in once with every camp session."

She laughed. "I'm wondering if you're wasting your time being a doctor when camp counselor is so definitely your calling."

"The way it is now, I've got the best of both worlds," he said, grinning.

"Yes, I think you do."

And he seemed so happy whichever world he was in. That was remarkable, and she wondered how he did it because all his worlds were so vastly different. It spoke of the quality of the man, she supposed. And Reid Adams was quality through and through.

Yes, Reid Adams was definitely the daddy she wanted for Megan. She knew that for certain and now all she had to do was find a way to convince him of it. After all, for a man who loved being in a family, like Reid did, one more child shouldn't matter to him. In fact, he should welcome the opportunity...she hoped.

"He's really a very nice man," Keera explained to Megan as she settled the child into the porch swing. The compound was empty this afternoon, except for a couple of volunteers puttering around in the gardens, and it surprised Keera how much she missed the activity that had surrounded her these past few days, even though she really hadn't been out into it very much. And the children. Yes, she actually did miss them as well.

"And a very good doctor. What I'm hoping is that I can convince him to take you in, then you could come here whenever he does, and you'd also have two sisters."

Of course, at her age Megan didn't understand all this. In fact, she was dozing off, her head resting on Keera's lap, so not only did she not understand, she also wasn't listening.

But for Keera, hearing her plan expressed aloud made it all the more real to her. While she couldn't keep this child, and social services didn't seem to be making any headway in placing her in a suitable situation, Megan was a sweet little girl who deserved better than this limbo she was in right now. Keera wanted the best for her, and every time she thought about that, the only thing that popped into her head was Reid. He *was* the best. But the arrangement had to be by his choice and not her persuasion. That much she was adamant about. Reid had to do the choosing.

Of course, that didn't preclude her from making the right choices for Megan that would help her get chosen for ever.

"So, what I have in mind is that tomorrow I'm going to go into town and ask him to watch you for a little while, so he can get to know you better now that you're not feeling so bad. Then the day after that I'll figure out a way to have him spend even more time with you. I think that, given the way he feels about children, once he gets to know you, he won't want you going into the foster-care system, the way I don't want you there either.

"So when that happens, I'm going to have to rely on you to turn on your girlish charms to help woo him into daddyhood thinking. Think that's a good plan?"

Of course, Megan didn't respond. She was now sound asleep, well past the dozing stage and into a deep slumber, with her breathing heavy and even. Smiling, Keera pushed back the blonde hair from Megan's forehead and lightly stroked her cheek. So much innocence, she thought. At that age, her own innocence had already been taken from her, by the way she'd lived, by the things she'd seen. She didn't remember being two, but life around her must have made its impression on her. Even on someone so young. Even on Megan.

"It's not going to be easy for you," she whispered, "but I'm going to make sure you get what you need. I promise, Megan. I may not be the one to take care of you, but I know who is. And you'll never, ever have to go into the foster-care system." Easy words, tough challenge. But as a child of the system herself, she knew the life she didn't want Megan to have. "I promise," she said again, as Megan curled up in a precious little ball, hugging a teddy bear. It was such a cozy sight, it almost made Keera wish she could be a part of something like it.

A flash of the two of them together crossed her mind... mother and daughter. Nice thought, but not practical for either of them. Especially not for Megan. And Keera knew better, knew and fully realized her potential as well as her limits, and understood that all this domesticity wasn't in her. Maybe in fantasy it might be there, but not in reality.

In some ways, she was her mother's daughter. At least in those aspects. Megan deserved so much better than that. So much better...

"You up to a short walk?" she asked Megan later, after she'd rocked her in the swing for an hour and had caught herself enjoying the relaxation. It wasn't something she did too often—simply sit and do nothing. Admittedly, it had been nice, just existing without an agenda or a to-do list. No patients to take care of, no worries. Just listening to the birds, taking in the magnificent scenery.

"Mommy," Megan whimpered in response. "Want Mommy."

"I know you do, sweetheart. I know you do. But right now you have to stay with me for a little while longer." She didn't know how to tell the child her parents were dead. Telling anyone a loved one had died was the worst, but in her world she dealt with adults. How to do it with a child, especially one so young, she didn't have a clue. "Let's walk over to the woods..." Instinctively, she felt the girl's forehead, not like a doctor but more like a mom, to see if she had a fever. Which she didn't. "Or we can go back inside. Whichever you want to do."

Megan didn't respond so Keera took her by the hand and led her off the porch and in the direction of the woods. She didn't expect to go very far, and was surprised how Megan resisted when she'd decided it was time to turn back. So they trudged on, only now Keera was carrying the child, pointing out the very few things she knew about nature...birds, flowers, trees, none identified by their proper name. But Megan was two, so Keera wasn't too concerned about that.

"Look at that tree," she said, putting Megan down and pointing to a giant pine. "It grows needles, not leaves. And pine cones." She bent to pick up a fallen pine cone then placed it in Megan's hands. "See how pretty that is? You can keep it if you want to."

Megan did look at the pine cone, clenching it tight in her little hands.

"That's the seed, Megan," she explained. "A whole tree can grow from that." She felt a little silly explaining that to a child too young to understand, but it seemed like the right thing to do. "You plant seeds in the ground, and they grow trees and bushes, even grass and flowers. But this one will grow a tree just like that one." She pointed to the pine. "Isn't it beautiful?"

"I'm surprised she's up to it," Reid called from the trail behind them.

Keera spun, surprised to see him there. "I thought you were rafting with the kids."

"They're rafting, I'm not. Sometimes I can be…overprotective, let's call it. The kids don't need a doctor hovering over them all the time, and that's really who I am to them. So I stayed through the picnic lunch and made sure they all understood what they were supposed to do. Then let some of the camp volunteers take charge. After that I left." He grinned. "And nobody noticed I was gone, they were so excited to get on the water."

"Poor Dr. Adams, feeling so under-appreciated," Keera teased. She glanced down at Megan, who was beginning to look weary, leaning hard against her leg and clinging. "I think you're going to be needed here shortly to carry her back, if that makes you feel any better."

"Needed maybe. But only for my brawn."

And a very nice brawn it was. "I'm surprised she's held up this long. But it's been fun, hasn't it, Megan?"

In response, Megan shrugged, then hugged her teddy bear and her pine cone even tighter. "She's missing…you-know-who."

"I expect she would be. So, what have you told her?"

"Me?" Keera exclaimed. "I can't tell her. I don't know how. I mean, she's too young to really understand, and I expect you've got to use the right words so you don't cause some sort of trauma that would pop up later in her life. So maybe her social worker will have a better idea of how to do it." *Or you,* she wanted to say. But she wouldn't be so presumptuous. Still, if he volunteered, she wouldn't turn him down.

"But she's been asking so she's going to have to know."

"That's one of the reasons I'm not suited to the job. I don't know what to do."

"Child experts say be honest and simple in your explanation."

Keera shook her head. "Not now. Maybe I'm not a child

expert, but I don't think telling her…well, you-know-what is a good idea when she's still not feeling well. There has to be a right time for it, and I suppose you play that by instinct."

"Which in you seems pretty good."

"Or resistant. Because I don't want to." She lowered her voice and whispered, "I don't want to break a little girl's heart."

"Maybe you're right."

"I know I'm right, Reid. Now's not the time."

"Then I bow to your instinct, because it's better than you think. Look, I'm going to run down to the river, it's only a few hundred yards, and wave to the kids as they float by, then we'll go back to the infirmary."

He scooped Megan into his arms, and urged Keera to follow him. "Just because they don't need me hovering doesn't mean I can't hover a little bit. Right, Megan?" he asked the child.

She responded by pressing her head to his chest, and it looked right. Like they were meant to be together. In fact, it looked so right it gave Keera some hope that her plan might just work.

Reid knew exactly what Keera was up to. She wanted him to fall in love with Megan then keep her. It was a good plan, and so far Keera wasn't pursuing it too aggressively, for which he was grateful because while the idea of adopting other children had crossed his mind more than once, he wasn't sure if he was ready for it. But he knew that's what Keera wanted, even though she was about as subtle in her pursuits as anyone he'd ever seen. It was there, though, in her eyes, in the way she looked at him, the way she looked at Megan. Good heart in the right place, but a heart that was a little trussed up.

Whatever the case, he had faith in her maternal instincts—more than she did, apparently. So he'd go along with her plan for a while, let her continue to think she was pursuing him, but take every opportunity that presented itself to turn that around on her without her knowing he was doing it, and pursue her into mommyhood.

Now, that was the perfect plan.

Could he take in Megan, though, if his plan failed? Adopt her, make her his third child? Maybe that was something to consider, a second-best plan. God knew, he knew how to raise a two-year-old. That, and his girls were secure, so in his future he could see fitting one or two, maybe three more children into his family.

In fact, he'd already approached his daughters with the idea, and they'd put in their order for all girls. Dr. Reid Adams and his half-dozen or so daughters. It brought a smile to his face. And since he wasn't rushing toward the altar any time soon, adoption seemed the best way to make that large-family dream happen. Then if, somewhere down the line, some woman wanted him, and his daughters...

But that wouldn't be Keera, by her own admission, so he was steering clear of her in that regard, as much as he didn't want to. Steering clear and hoping to hell he could keep his head, his wits, and even his sanity, because Keera was... He thought about all the things he wanted and she was all of them except for the one thing. *And that one thing was huge*. She didn't want to be a mother. For him a family with lots of kids wasn't negotiable, especially as he had already started on the course and was loving it.

"Here they come," he said to Megan, as three big, yellow rubber rafts came floating gently around the bend in the river. "Can you wave to them, Megan?" To help her, he raised her right hand and waved it for her.

"Looking good!" he shouted, as the first raft of children waved and yelled at him. They were all animated, yelling, clapping, wearing orange life-vests and black helmets, having the time of their lives. Briefly, Reid glanced over at Keera, who stood there unaffected, her arms folded across her chest. Staring at the…well, not at the children. And not at Megan. "Bet I can beat you to the next turn in the river," he shouted.

"Can't," one of the boys shouted back.

"Can too," he shouted in return, then passed Megan back to Keera. "Looks like I've got to take up the challenge. Sorry, but I think you're going to have to carry her back to the clinic. She looks like she could stand a good nap, probably sooner rather than later."

With that, he sprinted off into the trees, leaving Keera standing in the woods holding Megan in her arms. He didn't go too far, though. Just far enough that she couldn't see him duck behind a large tree and watch her turn and hike back to her cabin, toting one very heavy little deadweight.

"I'm on to you, Keera Murphy. And I know I'm right about you. Deny it all you want, but by the end of this week you're going to be that child's mother through and through."

OK, so maybe his talk was more confident than the way he actually felt, but in his heart he knew that if she only let herself go…

The shouts of the kids coming from downriver prised him away from watching her, and Reid turned and ran to his next rendezvous point. *"Yes, Keera,"* he said, as the kids floated into view, *"you're going to discover—"*

"Dr Adams!" came the unanimous shouts from the lead raft. "How'd you get here so fast?"

"Because I know how," he said, but not to the kids, as

his mind was still on Keera. Sure, he might know how with the kids, but did he know how with her?

Hell, he didn't even know why he wanted to know how. But he did. In a big way.

CHAPTER SIX

"I'LL BET YOU'LL be glad when life gets back to normal," Keera said, settling onto the porch swing outside the infirmary door, while Reid was seated in the chair across from it. "I really am sorry I'm disrupting you so much. I mean, you're not even getting to see your girls as much as you probably want to."

"Emmie and Allie are having the time of their lives without me hovering over them, which is what I usually do when I have the chance. And it's not like they were staying here with me in the first place."

"Yes, but you snuck in visits in your free time, and now you're barely getting any free time."

"Well, Emmie, I think, is particularly glad to get away from all that togetherness for a while. She's growing up, needs her space, even though I'm not ready to give it to her yet. Here, or back home in Sugar Creek. So you being here is a blessing in disguise for them."

"Knowing when to let go—one of the challenges of being a parent, I suppose."

"One of the many. Lately, though, the big thing has to do with fashion. I'm not good at it, don't have a clue. I remember the way my mom used to dress my sisters, but..."

"Old school," Keera chimed in. "I'll bet she dressed them old school. I mean, we come from a day when colors coordinated and matching patterns with similar patterns made sense. Now anything goes as long as it's fun. Nothing has to coordinate, nothing has to match if you feel good wearing it and it expresses…you."

"Don't I know. And what I'm finding out is that my daughter is hiding her clothes. *'Oh, Daddy, that's so gross,'* she always tells me. Then I never see the outfit again. Did you do that when you were a kid?"

"I never had enough clothes that I could hide something. But I definitely had my preferences." She smiled, remembering how she used to love window shopping.

She and her mom had never gone in to buy, and most of what she'd worn back then had been shoplifted from various thrift stores. It had always been her job to distract the store clerk while her mom had stuffed her coat with whatever she had been able to lift in mere seconds.

Usually it hadn't been pretty. Usually it hadn't even come close to fitting. Sometimes it had been in good shape, though, and she'd pretended it was brand-new. "Want me to take your girls shopping? Let them express themselves to me rather than having Daddy foist his taste on them?"

"I thought you'd never ask. How about after the zip line tomorrow afternoon? I'll sit with Megan then that will free you up to take the clothing nightmare away from me."

If ever a plan had played directly into her hands, this was it. How perfect was that? Leave him alone here, let him bond a little more with Megan…yes, perfect. "Well, I've never been shopping for kids' clothing, except that once for Megan, but it can't be that bad, can it?" she said, laughing.

"Just wait until tomorrow. Then you'll see."

"Well, call me crazy, but I think I might be looking forward to it."

"I know I am," he said, smiling. "And the girls will be excited to have some female input rather than letting dear old Dad horn in on their fashion creativity."

"This is where someone might normally make a profound parenting comment, offer condolences, or say something to the effect that you're better at it than you think, but as I don't have any experience in childhood situations or parenting, I don't think I'm qualified."

"Sounds like a cop-out to me. Especially when I'm clearly drowning and need a lifeline." He faked a pained expression. "Or sympathy."

"How about dinner? I'll cook. Not sure how, or where…"

"How about we spend our separate time with our respective girls then meet up later when they're all tucked in, and have our own meal?" Pausing, he smiled. "I don't know how my parents did it, taking care of so many kids going in so many directions and still finding time for themselves. But they did, and I guess I never even gave it any thought until now. Because the thing I'd like to do most is go for a walk, take you down to the river, have a late-night picnic and spend some time relaxing under the stars. But you have your responsibilities, I have mine, and those responsibilities come first."

"Would have been a nice evening, though," she said, trying not to sound too dreamy, or too disappointed. Because she could picture the evening playing out, and it was so real she almost felt immersed in it. But being immersed in an evening with Reid was a dangerous thing, because she was beginning to like him too much, and like was tantamount to love or other places she couldn't go. "But you're right, work and children come first," she said, shaking herself back into the true Keera Murphy mode.

"Maybe we could have sandwiches on the porch?"

"Or skip the sandwiches, and just spend some quiet time," she suggested.

"Quiet time is good, too. But what just happened here?" he asked. "How did we go from planning a meal together later on to whatever you just said?"

She laughed. "I was thinking in practical terms."

"And what about eating a meal together isn't practical, as we've already done it before?"

"The timing. After you do this, after I do that. Get the kids settled down, finish the day's worth of charting, plan tomorrow's class. Relaxing without a purpose after all that just seems nice. At home I'd just go straight to bed, but here relaxing seems almost required, doesn't it? You know, sit back, watch the stars, listen to the bullfrogs court their lady loves. Just breathe."

He pushed his glasses back up on his face and grinned. "Then it's a date to relax and breathe."

"You are different, Dr. Adams. Like nobody I've ever met before."

"Because men always want something else from you?"

Most of her life they had. Until she'd perfected her demeanor and polished her defenses. Which had started at a very young age, and had only gotten better over time. "Yes, to a point. I grew up in a situation where there were always men coming and going. So I got my fair share of looks, and I knew what they'd want, given the opportunity."

"Which makes you cautious."

"I try to be."

"Do you assume every man is giving you one of those looks?"

"Not every man. But I don't need to waste my time distinguishing between them because I'm not interested. Been there, failed miserably at it, saw every one of my character flaws exposed, and realized I can't go near it again."

"Said adamantly."

"Adamantly," she agreed. "But breathing is a practical matter and I'm looking forward to breathing with you later on." To show him her practicality in the matter, she leaned forward and extended her hand to shake his. But when his smooth palm glided across hers, it wasn't only his palm she felt. It was also the thousand impractical goose-bumps that were suddenly marching up and down her arms, up her neck, down her back.

His response was simply to arch his eyebrows at her then stand up and walk away.

And her response to that? More goose-bumps.

"She's what?" Keera asked, totally composed.

"Chest pains. Shortness of breath. Rapid pulse, elevated blood pressure. She's in her cabin, sitting on the couch, refusing to budge, and seeing as you're a cardiac specialist…"

"Surgeon," she corrected. "And I can't come because I'm the only one here to sit with Megan."

"And I can't leave Clara alone to trade places with you." So they were in a spot. He in one spot, she in another, and never the twain shall meet. Which also described their lives, it seemed. "Let me call Sally and send her over there."

Keera glanced over at Megan, almost hating to leave her. They'd been reading stories, having a nice evening together. "Then I'll get some supplies ready. You keep her head elevated, give her an aspirin."

"No aspirin. She's allergic."

"Fine, just try and keep her calm. Keep checking her vitals. Are either of your girls with you, by chance?"

"Emmie is. Why?

"Send Emmie over here, and I'll give her an IV set-up, plus whatever drugs I can scrounge for a cardiac episode. Is Clara coherent?" Clara, the camp cook.

"Very."

"That's good. So hang up. Call Sally and I'll—"

"Daddy sent me," Emmie said. She was standing in the doorway, a little out of breath from the hard run across the compound.

"So fast."

Emmie nodded. "Miss Clara is having a heart attack," she said so matter-of-factly it rattled Keera. It also reminded Keera a little of herself at that age—all seriousness, no innocence or typical childishness.

"Look, you go back out on the porch and wait. OK? We don't want to expose you to Megan's measles."

"Measles are a normal childhood disease," Emmie explained, without budging from the infirmary doorway, "but my daddy doesn't want me exposed to anything that will make me sick."

She raised a finger to Emmie to indicate she'd get back to her in a moment, then returned to Reid on the phone. "Look, Emmie's here, so I've got to go. I'll be there as fast as I can."

"Clara's not going to die, is she?" Emmie asked.

"We're going to do everything we can for her. Beginning with this." She grabbed a box of IV tubing and catheter, and a bag of normal saline from the supply closet. "Take this to your daddy."

"Could you talk to him, tell him I'm all better now? That he doesn't have to take care of me so much any more? Or keep worrying. That he needs to have some fun, because he doesn't. Not ever."

"He's asked me to take you and Allie shopping tomorrow. We'll talk about it then, OK?"

Emmie nodded on her way out the door, her arms full of medical supplies, and Keera stood there and watched her run across the compound to the cook's cabin. Only when she was inside did Keera leave the door and return to the locked drug supply to find whatever medication might be necessary to see Clara through her heart attack.

By the time Sally arrived, Keera had a fairly substantial bag packed, but before she left the cabin she took a moment to go over to Megan. "Look, I've got to go away for a little while. Sally's going to stay and read more stories to you, and I'll be back as soon as I can. I promise, Megan. I'll hurry back here as soon as I can."

"No," Megan said very quietly.

"I'm sorry, but I have to."

Big tears welled in Megan's eyes. Tears that surprisingly tore at Keera.

"She's going to be fine, Doctor," Sally said. "I'll get her settled down, and she'll be fine in no time."

"I hope so," Keera said, bending down to give the girl a kiss on the forehead. "But that doesn't make me feel any better."

"They're resilient at this age. Bounce back from disappointment very quickly."

Maybe they bounced back, but did they get over it? That's what worried Keera about Megan, because she had so much to get over in her young life. More than any child her age should have to worry about.

"Oh, and if you don't mind, as soon as Megan dozes off, I'm going to do the same in the bed next to hers. So take the night off if you'd like, because I don't intend to budge from this place until morning."

"Are you sure?"

"It's hard to keep up with these kids. I love them to death, but they're wearing me out. That bed there is looking pretty inviting."

"Call me if you change your mind."

"Not going to happen," she said, sitting down on the edge of the bed with Megan. "Trust me, five minutes after Megan's having pleasant dreams, I will be too."

Keera gave the older woman a hug then headed to the door. But she took one look back before she left, saw Megan watching her. And she felt…just like a mother for an instant. A mother torn between her child and her duty. Which was why she couldn't be a mother for real, because duty would always have to win.

Sighing, Keera stepped out into the night then flew across the compound and entered Clara's cabin, to be greeted by Reid, who was wearing a troubled expression.

"She's not…?" Keera asked, stepping into the tiny entry hall.

He shook his head. "We've got it sorted out and I'm pretty sure it's indigestion. But I'm going to send her to the hospital to be looked at anyway."

"Then why the grim face?"

"Emmie told me she came into the infirmary and saw Megan."

"Just in the doorway. Which is probably not close enough to have been exposed, especially as she's up to date on her vaccinations."

"How could you have let that happen, Keera? You know I don't want these kids exposed—"

"I didn't *let* it happen," she interrupted, whispering because she could see Emmie and Allie peeking out of the next room at them. "She came in, I gave her the supplies and she left. It took place over the course of about a minute."

"She shouldn't have been in there for a full minute. Don't you understand? She's vulnerable. All the kids are vulnerable, with compromised immune systems in many cases, and I shouldn't have—"

"What? Let me stay? You shouldn't have let me stay? Because you're right. You shouldn't have, and I shouldn't have accepted when you offered. But you did, and I did, and as a result Emmie was exposed to measles. She's healthy now, though. You're the one who said it."

"Healthy now doesn't mean she still doesn't have immunity problems. She does, and she's very susceptible to colds and flu and…measles."

"And her daddy's phobias. She wants to talk to me about it, Reid. She's pretty upset that you want to keep her so isolated. And I must say I'm impressed at the level on which she communicates. It's very adult. Maybe too adult." She looked past him, saw the girls still peeking out. "Like this. Suppose Clara *was* having a heart attack. They're in there, watching it. Did you know that? Talk about your daughters being exposed to something they shouldn't be."

He spun round in time to see his daughters scamper off into the kitchen. Then he went after them, took them to the rear bedroom in Clara's cottage and shut the door. "So you're giving me parenting advice now?" he said, once he'd returned to the front room.

"Not parenting advice. Just telling you that you can't always predict parenting the way you can't predict life. And also telling you what I think she's afraid to say to you. Emmie wants you to have your own life, Reid. She's worried that you don't because you're so fixated on her. I used to worry about my mother—all the bad things she did, all the bad situations she ended up in.

"I was too young to worry like that and Emmie's too

young to worry about you the way she does. But it's up to you, as the parent, to change that for her."

"Easier said than done."

"Maybe so, but I'm right. And this is something I understand better than most. Look, you go wait with your daughters and reassure them about Clara's condition, and I'll give you a second opinion about her heartburn. Then you can take the girls back to their dorm for the evening, and as Sally's settling in with Megan for the night, I'll fix us a late dinner. If you haven't eaten?"

He smiled. "You're back to cooking for me?"

"You've had a rough evening. It's the least I can do." With that, she pushed past him into the living room, where Clara was sitting up on the couch with her feet propped up and an ice pack on her head. "Dr. Adams said he believes you're suffering from indigestion. Mind if I take a look?"

Clara motioned her over to the couch. "I cook healthy for the kids, but I don't always eat my own cooking. Looks like those burritos got me this time."

Keera sat down next to Clara, took her pulse, blood pressure, listened to her heart. Blood pressure high, heart sounded fine. "The thing about burritos is they're good in moderation. But when your indigestion gets so bad it can be confused with a heart attack, that's when you have to reconsider your eating choices. Otherwise next time it could be a heart attack, which you might ignore because you think it's only indigestion again.

"And I don't want you ending up on my operating table, Clara. The kids here need you, need the way you cook for them and take such good care of them. So you owe it to yourself to take as good of care of yourself as you do them."

"I've never been a skinny person, Doctor," she said, sniffling. "I come from large stock."

"You can be large and still be healthy." She patted the woman's hand. "And I don't think you'd look right being skinny. Look, I don't know if Dr. Adams mentioned this, but we want to admit you to the hospital for the night for some tests. Just to make sure it's not cardiac related. If it is, they'll get you taken care of. If it isn't, and you're up to it, you can come back to camp tomorrow."

"What about breakfast and lunch? Somebody's got to do the cooking."

"Don't worry about the cooking. I know my way around a kitchen, if that's what I have to do."

"But we have different diets for different kids."

"If it's written down, I can read. All I want you to do is rest and let the doctors at the hospital take care of you. We'll figure out everything else tomorrow. OK?"

"You're not cold, like they're saying you are," Clara said, as the ambulance pulled up to the front of the cabin.

"Who says I'm cold?"

"Allie, but it came from Doc Reid. Only Allie interpreted it as meaning you needed a blanket."

"He thinks I'm cold?"

"That's what you want him to think, isn't it? You do kind of put it on, you know."

Maybe it *was* what she wanted him to think. Maybe it was the way she wanted the entire world to see her. Because there was safety in that frostiness. But it hurt, hearing someone say it out loud, because she wasn't cold deep down. She knew that. If only Reid knew that as well.

"So, what's the plan?" Reid asked. She was puttering around Reid's cabin kitchen. Looking pretty good at it. But she looked pretty good at everything she did.

"Looks like I'm going to be the camp cook until Clara gets back," she said, trying to sound as cold as he thought she was. "So I'm going to go over there right now and familiarize myself with the kitchen. Oh, and about that dinner I promised you." She pointed to a sandwich on a plate, sitting there alongside a glass of milk.

"That's it?"

"That's it," she confirmed in her best, and iciest, voice.

"You're angry because you've got to cook?"

"No, I'm angry because you decided it was necessary to discuss my cold demeanor with your daughter, who discussed it with the camp cook." Facing him, she leaned back against the counter and folded her arms across her chest. "Cold! Really? Is that what you think of me?"

"How about cold by design?"

"I'm not a cold person, Reid. Maybe reserved but not—"

"I didn't mean to offend you."

"Because you didn't think it would get back to me."

"There's that. But it was something mentioned the first night you were here."

"So this is where you're going to tell me you've changed your mind?" she asked.

If anything, she was blazing hot tonight, and sexy as hell. "Look, you're not an ice maiden but you do put on this air of chilliness. Which, by the way, I don't think is the real you."

"But why mention it to your daughter?"

"I was irritated that you'd barged in and disrupted my entire life, not to mention my camp. So I may have spoken in haste, called you a cold…"

"A cold what?" she asked.

"It wasn't meant for little ears. She accidentally overhead."

"A cold what?" Keera persisted.

"And I corrected myself, and left her with the impression you were cold, as in temperature-wise."

"A cold what?" she asked again. "Let me hear you say the word."

"OK. I called you a cold bitch, because I knew your intention was to leave Megan here and walk away. And I meant it. For a few minutes. Now I apologize, because I was wrong."

"Because you got caught?" she questioned, fighting back a smile. He was kind of cute, trying to worm his way out of this one. He definitely looked like the little boy who'd got caught doing something he wasn't supposed to, and she couldn't help but be more endeared than enraged.

"Clara's fine," he said, trying to change the subject.

"She doesn't think I'm cold."

"We're back to that?"

"We never got off it." Walking to the fridge to put away the milk, she brushed past him and paid particular attention to their proximity because she didn't want to touch him, didn't want another epidemic of goose-bumps. But the intensity between them was suddenly making her nervous. She could feel the heat of his stare on the back of her neck, which was where her goose-bumps began again. Oh, to be cold at this precise moment, because she was feeling anything but.

How could any man make her so acutely aware of herself? Make her feel so self-conscious? Make her feel so vulnerable to thoughts she didn't even know he was having? But that she herself definitely was having?

In truth, he was awakening something in her that was a complete and messy surprise. Did she want this man? In the physical sense she was almost willing to admit she might. She was only human and, God knew, she did come with those needs like everybody did. Only she fought harder to keep them under control. So the really messy part here was how he'd got through the barriers.

Thankfully, she still had her controls in place so he'd only get so far. Which was as far as goose-bumps and a few straying thoughts.

"What I think is that you show me exactly what you want me to see, and believe. What I also think is that maybe you kid yourself about what you feel, even about who you are. Don't know why, not going to guess." He grabbed her arm and pulled her back to him. "But I have a confession of my own to make. I'm attracted to you. And when you talked about men looking at you…I looked."

She looked up into his eyes. Swallowed hard. "But we can control the urges, Reid."

"Because we want to or because we have to?"

Nothing in her wanted to because she liked the way he held her—his grip not rough yet not gentle. And she liked his dominance. It was firm but not unrelenting. "Because it's the only practical thing to do."

"Depends on your definition of practical," he said, pulling her up roughly against his chest.

Keera looked up, put her hands on the sides of his face to hold him where she wanted him, which was no place but here, in this moment. Then she wound her fingers up through his hair, tugged it slightly and smiled when he started to breathe faster. Breaths to match hers. The edges of their bodies melted into each other.

Keera's body ached from a terrible emptiness, one never before filled, and she was so acutely aware of Reid, more than she had ever been of anything or anyone else in her life. The way he looked down over the tops of his glasses at her—glasses that she removed and laid on the kitchen countertop. How his light evening stubble felt under her fingertips. But what made her quiver, as she explored his face, was the slight dent in the center of his bottom lip. And that discovery about him, and about herself was where the exploration stopped and the kiss began.

In that instant their mouths pressed together hot and tight as his free hand entwined through her hair. Gasping when he eased her head back and kissed down her chin, down her throat, she responded by putting her palms flat to his chest, as if to push him away. Only she gripped the fabric of his shirt, two hands clinging tight to him, feeling the muscles underneath. Hard, smooth… "We shouldn't," she gasped.

"And we won't," he agreed, without retreating a step. "In a minute."

The growl of his sex-charged voice was heavy and hypnotic to her ears and just the sound of it caused her whole body to ache like she'd never known it could. A betrayal of sense and soul, and she fought to get it back, but as his kisses returned to her mouth, all she could do was kiss him back. And hang on for fear she might drown if she didn't.

But all too soon reality overtook the moment, in the form of a jingling cellphone, the jingle being the specific one he'd assigned Emmie, and Reid stepped back, cleared his throat, and assumed the role of daddy.

"What do you want, sweetheart?" He listened for a moment. "No, like I told you a little while ago, it wasn't a heart attack. She'll be fine. I just talked to them at the hospital and she'll be back tomorrow afternoon. And, yes, I did feed her dog. He's outside right now, and I'll bring him in when I go to bed." Another moment of listening, then, "I love you too, sweetheart. Tell Allie I love her, too. Then turn off the cellphone and go to sleep."

Once he'd clicked off, Reid grinned sheepishly. "So, is this where we ignore what happened and go on like we were?"

"It was a kiss," she said, her voice sounding wobbly. "Just a kiss."

"Just a kiss," he said, picking up his peanut-butter sandwich. "Between colleagues."

Keera nodded, trying to appear practical about the matter. "A kiss between colleagues." And one that had shaken her to the very core. Which meant what?

That was the question she didn't want to answer.

CHAPTER SEVEN

"I DON'T WANT to do this," Keera said, as the instructor secured her into the zip-line harness. "I'm fine keeping my feet on the ground. Never did have a need to simply go flying through the air without an airplane around me. And I don't like all this protective gear..." Harness, pads, goggles. "It pinches, and I especially don't like helmets."

"Necessary for safety and insurance. And it sets a good example for the kids. Especially when you're not fussing and fretting about it," Reid said, then took a picture of her with all her gear.

"But I am fussing and fretting," she said, looking over at Megan, who was sitting under a tree with Sally a good distance away from the rest of the children. "And complaining outright, as it wasn't my idea to do this."

Reid laughed out loud. "Like I said, you have to set a *good* example for the kids. They're watching you, you know."

Yes, they were all watching her, so she pasted a smile on her face and gave them a thumbs-up sign. "It's all a lie," she said under her breath. "I don't like this, don't want to do it."

"Role model," he reminded her, nodding sideways in a gesture toward to the kids. "They have high expectations of you. Even Megan does."

"Megan's too young to understand most of this, and why would the others expect anything from me?" she asked, as the instructor cinched the harness tighter.

"Because they like you, and trust you."

"Then they don't know me," she said, scooting her elbow pads into place then pulling her goggles down over her eyes. "And the last thing I want to be is a role model. Too much responsibility, especially when children are involved. They need someone like you, not like me." And she'd survived perfectly well without a role model in her own life. Or with the worst role model a child could have, depending on how you looked at it.

"Too late for that. You've been thrust into greatness, Keera, as far as these kids are concerned, and there's no turning back. They trust you, respect you and even look up to you. And your confidence in them learning to take responsibility for themselves has made you more of a role model than you can know, because these kids have never had someone who trusts them that much. Not even me."

"It wasn't trust. It was practicality. And you know how that governs my life. It should govern theirs as well, as far as their health issues are concerned."

"But they don't see it that way. To them, it's a very personal thing, making you their—"

"Role model," she said, tightening the chin strap of her helmet then bending over to adjust her knee pads. Taking a quick look at the kids out of the corner of her eye, she saw the way they were watching her, and realized every last word Reid had said was true. Which made her feel uncomfortable for sure, yet strangely moved. "Fine, I'll do this, and I won't make a scene. But I may have to scream, and there's nothing you can do about that."

"I'll bet the kids will love that."

"Yeah, right," she said, turning to the group of kids

now that she was all garbed up and taking a proper bow. Only to be met by applause and shouts of excitement. "And if I die…"

"You're not going to die," he said, walking her over to the platform.

"But if I do…"

"Then I'll be properly put in my place, and you can come back and haunt me, and tell me *you told me so.*"

"And I will," she said, as she began her climb up the wooden ladder nailed onto the post holding up the zip-line platform. "I promise you, Reid Adams, I will haunt you until your dying day."

He'd tossed and turned a bit last night, thanks to the kiss. But somehow he'd finally settled down into a sound sleep and had slept like a cozy baby. In two-hour stretches, as he was up and down, gazing across the compound at Keera's light, wondering if she was sleeping or if the kiss had her tossing and turning as well.

So far that morning they'd been only colleagues and sparring partners. She'd cooked breakfast for the kids while he'd done morning rounds. He'd cleaned up the kitchen while she'd taught her class on taking vital statistics. Then they'd met to collaborate on preparing lunch, and now this. So far there was nothing personal between them. In fact, it was almost like last night hadn't happened. But it had, and there was no denying it. Short, intense and unforgettable. The best kiss he'd ever had.

Looking up, he watched her finally make it to the platform and wave over to Megan, then he pointed his camera up and snapped another picture, and turned it on to video record.

"Seriously, Reid? Do you have to record every aspect of my total, abject humiliation?" she yelled down to him.

Laughing, he stepped back to get a better, wider shot

of the whole event about to take place. "Total and abject is when you get halfway across the line and can't go on, and someone has to come and rescue you."

"You did that?"

"No. But I'm just saying…"

"You're just saying it to put the onus on me."

"But I'll have a video."

She glanced down at all the kids, who were much more eager to do the zip line than she was. "One time, then I'm taking Megan back to camp."

"What if you enjoy it?"

"I won't!"

"That sure of yourself?" he yelled.

"That sure of myself. I *will not* enjoy this."

"Then shall we make a wager? If I win, you take me out to dinner. You win and…well, name your prize. Within reason."

"If I win? I'll have to think about it."

"Don't bother. I'm going to win this bet."

"That sure of yourself, are you?"

He shook his head. "No, but I'm that sure of you."

He watched Keera position herself on the platform and take last-minute instructions. Then he saw her hesitation as the instructor hooked her to the line and she inched towards the edge of the platform. It wasn't such a high wire. In fact, he'd gone zipping on higher, much more extensive wires. Zipped over canopies of trees, skimmed along mountains. Taken an all-day outing once, combining zipping and hiking. All that had been back before he'd become a dad, and had had dad responsibilities.

Sometimes he did miss that freedom. Wondered what it would be like to share his parental responsibility with someone so he could afford a little time away. Mostly, though, he loved the responsibility, loved everything that came with it.

Although, after last night, some of the longing had returned—longing he'd put on hold the day he'd made his decision to adopt the girls. Well, it was good to know it was still there. Unfortunately, it was now dusted off and raring to go, and as long as Keera was here, it wasn't going to go back into storage. The fifty or so photos of her he'd taken already, and now the video, were proof enough of that.

"Do you seriously think I'm going to step off this platform?" she called down to him.

"Want me to come up there and give you a push?"

"What I want is an activity where I can keep both feet planted firmly on the ground. Something sane, like taking a hike. Or jogging."

"One step, Keera. That's the way everything starts in life. With one step." And she needed that step because she did keep everything so locked up.

She looked down at him again then looked over at the kids, and shrugged. Then took that step, to the shouts and screams of the children, who were jumping up and down, applauding her. In a few seconds she was on the opposite platform, raising her arms in the air in victory. Waving at the kids. Shouting her own glee at the task completed.

"I didn't hear you scream," he said, showing her the playback of the video.

"Because it happened so fast. One moment my feet were on solid ground then the next I was flying."

"See, I told you." he said, helping her off with her helmet. "Want to do it again?"

"Think I could?"

"We have two hours here. I'll bet you can do it several more times."

"That was…" She smiled. "Pick your restaurant, Reid.

You win. You were right. So revel in it now, because that's all you're getting from me. One admission and one only. It was fun. I loved it."

"One admission leading to one dinner but an admission with so much significance. Because victory is sweet. Trust me, one is all I need from you." And maybe another kiss at the end of the evening. But he wasn't going to hope too hard for that. Once was pushing it, twice would be... well, very nice, but also a very long long-shot. Still, long-shots were good to bet on because when they won, they paid off big.

"I'll talk to him, but I can't promise he'll like anything we've bought today." They'd been shopping for two hours, and the clothes were cute. Not traditional, not frilly. More like bright, and fun, lots of colors, lots of layers. And accessories. Oh, my heavens, his daughters were starved for accessories. Apparently their daddy was quite practical in some aspects of his personality, and allowing his daughters to express their true creativity was one of those aspects.

When they'd hit the accessories aisle of the little girls' section in the boutique where she'd shopped for Megan, it had been like a whole new world had opened up for Emmie and Allie. Bows and matching socks, purses, belts. And shoes to match specific outfits. These girls lived in basic colors and basic sneakers. Red and pink shoes were entirely new to them, and she couldn't quit buying.

In a way, a whole new world was opening to her, too. Partly because of Megan, and partly because of Emmie and Allie. It was so much unexpected fun, like the zip line. It was also all the things of which she'd been deprived when she'd been a girl that were coming back to remind her now, and she was regaining, vicariously, some of what

she'd never had. Even now, her own shopping was practical, quick, and of necessity. And always, always basic.

But this…instead of regretting her past and even parts
of her present life, she was enjoying every minute of the
outing with Reid's daughters, and being ever mindful that
Megan could be part of this in the near future, if all went
well.

Also wishing Megan could be part of it now. She truly
would have liked to include her.

"Was your daddy like that?" Emmie asked innocently,
as she plowed through the section of hair accessories, looking for individual pieces to match each of the six outfits
she'd picked out so far. "Like my daddy is?"

"I never got to know my daddy," Keera said. "He went
away before I was born."

"He's lost?" Allie asked.

"I suppose you could say he is. But I don't think he
wanted any little girls the way your daddy does."

"Would he want you if you were a boy?" Allie asked.

Keera laughed. "No, honey. I don't think he would.
Some people don't want to be mommies or daddies."

"Like you?" Emmie asked, picking out a green and
yellow hair bow. "I heard you and daddy talking and you
said you didn't want children."

"You don't want Megan?" Allie asked.

This really wasn't the conversation she wanted to be
having with the girls but apparently it was the conversation they wanted with her. "I like children. I like both of
you a lot. Megan, too. But I work almost every day, all
day, and I wouldn't have time to be a good mommy, and
Megan needs a good…" Well, she was hoping for a daddy,
but how could she say that to these two?

"She needs a good home where someone's there to take
care of her more than I could. Look, would either of you

like ice cream?" That was the way to do it. When the situation got tough, cure it with ice cream. Yet another reason she wasn't cut out for motherhood. Simply put, she was stuck for what to do.

How in the world did Reid do this day in, day out? It was beyond her, and she realized she admired him not only for wanting to do this but for being good at it. And as she ordered two chocolate cones and a dish of strawberry, she realized even more that this was where Megan needed to be.

"They had a great time," Reid said. "I'm not sure about their—or your—fashion choices. But I suppose I'll get used to that, won't I? And I really insist on paying you back for everything you bought."

"Donate the money to the camp. I want this to be my treat."

"Because you're a surgeon who earns more than a county pediatrician?"

"Actually, I'm sure I do. Which isn't the point. We had a nice time and I thoroughly enjoyed the afternoon. So, please, don't spoil it by being..."

"Practical?" he asked, smiling.

"You're using my own life to prove me wrong?"

"You're the one who insists on being practical. So what can I say?"

"I can say that you've done a good job with the girls. I'm impressed you manage it all so well. Your life, your work, your parental responsibilities..."

"I manage it because I want to. It's all about priorities, I suppose. You know, the overall priorities, then the moment-to-moment priorities."

"And I manage my surgical practice the way I want to,

so I guess that pretty much tells you everything there is to know about my priorities."

"Which will never change?" he asked.

"Which I don't anticipate will change. Don't want to change."

"Even if your life situation changes?"

"Another thing I don't anticipate or want." Pulling into the parking spot of The Overlook, she looked at the building and almost wished she'd chosen the restaurant. This place was so romantic. Too romantic maybe? Rustic, and with a view the literature said couldn't be topped anywhere in the vicinity. And in the aftermath of that kiss. What was she thinking?

That she was flirting with things best left alone. That's what she was thinking. But this time she was better prepared. She knew she succumbed too easily to, well, it was either his charm or the clean mountain air, or the moment, or any number of the other reasons two people found that fleeting mutual attraction. And it was only fleeting. Had to be! She was going to make sure of that or she wasn't Keera Murphy, the cold bitch. Make that the *stone*-cold bitch.

But darn it. Once she stepped inside the restaurant, saw the dimmed lights, heard the violin music, her knees nearly buckled. And they really did buckle when she and Reid were shown to the table with the best view in the restaurant, and she had to hold on to that table for support. It was stunning at twilight, with the pinks and grays of the evening sky peeking over the distant mountains. "How did you manage this?" she asked Reid.

"Owners' names are Gwen and Henry Carson."

"As in Gregory Carson?"

He nodded. "They've struggled to hang onto the place, with all their medical expenses. Amazing people, though. They do it all, and take care of a recovering kid, too."

"So this is going to be another exercise in how I could or should be a parent, even with my circumstances, and the Carsons are going to show me the way? Is that why we're here? It's an object lesson?"

"No, but they are going to serve you one of the most amazing meals you've probably ever had."

"Which is meant to prove that I, too, can be a super-mom, like you're a super-dad, and they're super-parents?"

Suddenly, she had no desire to be here, no desire to spend the evening with her face being rubbed in her inadequacies. Sure, she felt guilty about Megan. Her feelings for the little girl were growing. She liked taking care of her, reading her stories, taking walks with her, playing games. But that was largely due to the circumstances—she was out of her element, living a life that wasn't hers. And now, with so many people trying to prove the point, she wasn't comfortable any more. Didn't want to be here, being forced to face the obvious.

So she wasn't going to stay and subject herself to that, no matter how the evening was *intended*. It was as simple as that. Reid could stay, and she'd leave the money to pay for it because nowhere in that bet had there been a mention of dinner for two. Or an object lesson on essential parenting guidelines, which this was all about.

Was she angry? Maybe a little. Or feeling guilty? Probably some of that thrown in there as well. Because she couldn't do it all and she knew it. Knew her inadequacies and didn't have to be reminded of them over the soufflé. But she also knew her strengths, one of which wasn't going to be the commendable kind of parent Reid, or even the Carsons, were. So she pulled her credit card from her purse, slapped it down on the table, and said, "Enjoy yourself. Don't hold back and, please, just slip the card under my cabin door when you return to camp." With that, Keera spun around and marched straight out of the restaurant, quite sure she could hear Reid following her. But she wouldn't turn around to look, not even when she got to the car and had to pause a moment to find the key fob in her purse.

"It was supposed to be a simple dinner," he said. "I'm not sure what you read into it that turned it into something else, but I'm sorry if I said the wrong thing."

"There's not one wrong thing," she said. "Everything's wrong. A week ago I didn't know this camp or you existed, and Megan was only a name and not a child with real-life needs. And this time next week I'll have my real life back and this whole mountain fantasy where I end up being mom of the year will be over and I'll have my elbows up in somebody's rib cage, repairing their heart. It's all I can do, Reid." She looked up at him.

"All I'm supposed to do. It's the reality where I control my life and everything in it. And it's where I don't feel guilty because I can't do the noble thing, the way you can."

"Control is that important you?"

"It has to be. Or else I end up…like this." She spread her arms to take in the whole expanse of town that could be viewed from their vantage point.

"What's so bad about this?"

"For you, nothing. For me, everything. Absolutely everything." She drew in a steadying breath and leaned back against the car. "You were right, you know. I am cold. Because I want to be cold. It keeps the world from intruding, and it keeps me in the place I need to be. Where I belong."

"Which is alone."

"Which is unaffected. I know you want me to be that little girl's mother, or at least her guardian until a permanent home can be found for her."

"That's true."

She laughed, but it was a bitter laugh. Or one filled with regret. "You sound like your daughters. The subject came up when we were shopping and I think they were amazed that I couldn't step in and rescue Megan the way you stepped in and rescued them. But being the good role model that I am, I distracted them with ice cream because I didn't know what to say. So tell me, does the person who takes the low road really sound like the best candidate for motherhood?"

"She sounds like me when I struggle to find the right way to go. There's no book with all the answers you'll ever need to know, Keera. Not about parenting, not about life in general. But it works out, one way or another."

"For me, it works out when I'm scrubbed and ready to step into the OR."

"Having a child doesn't mean you can't do that."

"You don't know me, then. In my life all I can do is one thing. Look, dinner here was a bad idea because this place…you…Gregory's parents…suffocate me with my inadequacies. And I'm really not hungry. So, please, go back, have a nice evening on me. I'm sure you can catch a taxi back to the cabin. Or I can catch a taxi and leave you the car. However you want to work it out."

"Why do I scare you so much?" he asked.

There were so many reasons on so many levels, but most of all he reminded her of the things she'd never be able to have. Reid was everything, he had everything. And she was a shell. She knew that, and was OK with it. "You don't. I'm the one who scares me."

"Because of this?" he asked, tilting her face up to his. "Because you don't want to want it?"

With that, he lowered his lips to hers, but it was not a kiss filled with fire and raw need. It was tender, and gentle. Filled with hope she so desperately wanted to feel. Wanted to hold on to. "We shouldn't do this," she said, hating that she had to pull away from him. But she had to, because she so feared getting lost in the very thing she knew she couldn't have yet was only now beginning to realize she desperately wanted.

"You're right," he said, smiling. "We shouldn't. But once wasn't enough."

"Why do you even want to…well, do anything with me? Nothing can come of it."

"Or everything, depending on your perspective."

She shook her head. "There's only one perspective, and I think maybe the mountain air's gone to your head, Reid. Or perhaps you need more adult companionship. I don't know which. But have you thought this through? If nothing else, think of our proximity. We live more than an hour away from each other."

"Half an hour if we meet in the middle."

"And neither of us have that hour or half-hour to spare. And in the end we're too different."

"And opposites never attract."

"Not in reality," she said.

"So then why do I want to kiss you so badly, and why do you want me to?" he asked, clearly on the verge of their next kiss. "And we're pretty much opposite in everything?"

"Too many children around, and I'm back to believing you're craving some adult companionship."

"So, any adult will do, right? Any set of lips? Any curvy, sexy-as-hell hips…"

"Hmm," she murmured, as his lips met hers, but this time with a hunger that no romantic meal was going to satisfy.

"Wow," she said groggily, rolling over and looking at the naked body stretched out next to her. She certainly hadn't expected what was lurking beneath his clothing. Reid had a magnificent body, lean and well muscled. As a doctor, she knew physical perfection. As a woman, she'd never known she could enjoy it so much. Every inch of it. "Time to get up, leave this hotel and get back to camp, before anybody notices that we're missing."

"What time is it?"

"A little after one. And even though Sally is always happy to watch Megan, I want to spend the rest of the night with her. Which means we've got to go back to camp before it gets any later and people start wondering if we're doing what we just did." She smiled. "And I mean it, Dr. Adams. Appearances are important."

He reached over and twined his fingers through her hair. "I never knew how much I liked red hair before last night. But I definitely like red hair."

"I know," she said, not sure whether to be bold or opt for being demure.

"Nice red hair."

She sighed. "Seriously. We've got to go, Reid. Somebody's going to find out." She sat up and pulled the sheet up to cover her breasts, but he immediately reached over and tugged the sheet back down.

"I like your breasts as much as I like your hair. If you're going to kick me out of your bed, the least you could do is give me one last look."

She liked being admired, liked that it was Reid doing the admiring. "Technically, I'm not kicking. Just urging." And, oh, how she didn't want to. But getting here had been such a fluke, and then discovering how good they were together? Suffice it to say he'd melted the stone-cold bitch into a puddle, and she wasn't ready to have that end. But, practically speaking, it had to. Because they weren't practical together. Neither was this relationship. A few hours together were good, but anything beyond that… "And if you're not going to avail yourself of the shower, I will."

"Please, avail away. But leave the sheet here, because as much as I like your red hair and your breasts, well, all I can say is that watching you walk away from me, naked, is my fondest fantasy. Well, one of them."

His grin was wicked, his demeanor sexy and funny— everything she'd always wanted and had never had. Still couldn't have, and that's the only thing she could think of as she gave him his show on her way into the shower. She couldn't have any of this.

In another few minutes it would be over, and it all would be relegated to the past tense and dreams to be put away on the shelf. But no regrets. She was a modern woman, and modern women had flings. It was accepted. Something totally different from her mother's life and lifestyle. Although this was the first time she'd ever slept with a man outside marriage, which meant…

Actually, she wasn't going to ponder that one. No, she was going to take a shower and go about her plans for the rest of the night, and let Reid worry about what to tell his children, or anybody else for that matter, if he lolly-gagged too much and they didn't get back to camp at a respectable time.

But a little while longer in bed with him would have been nice. Sighing, Keera turned on the shower full blast and stepped in, and let the water pellets ping her skin a little harder than she usually did because she'd felt alive in his arms these last hours, and now she wanted something else to make her feel alive. Only a few minutes away from Reid and she needed a physical reminder…

"What have I done?" she whispered as she sank back against the shower wall and let the water beat hard against her.

"Room for one more?" he asked, snapping her out of her reverie.

"We shouldn't," she said, desperately wanting to anyway. "Because after tonight…" Keera shrugged.

"What? We're done?"

"We should be."

Reid turned on the grin. "Because we're not practical?"

"Something like that," she said, as he pushed back the shower curtain and entered. "I don't do this. Tonight, you and me. It's not me."

Picking up the bottle of body wash, he raised it and squeezed so that the pink soap inside slithered down between her breasts, all the way to her belly, and below. Then he began to spread the soap, the palms of both his hands making a circular motion on her flesh that left her gasping for breath. "Oh, this is definitely you," he said, taking particular care to tweak her nipples to erection then linger there, stroking, pinching lightly, then returning to his circular motion as his hands continued on their journey, down her belly, and even further down, until one hand forged ahead and the other hand reached around to grab her bottom.

"Reid, no." She gasped, "We shouldn't."

"Go on," he urged. "We shouldn't what?"

"Stop," she choked out, as the paroxysms of his efforts began to overtake her.

"Now? You want me to stop now?"

"No!" she practically screamed. "We shouldn't stop. Not now! Please, don't."

"As if I could," he growled, as she quivered beneath his fingertips. "Or would."

But they would have to at some point. That's what she was thinking when their shower was over, and an hour later when, car lights off, they drove into the camp and parked behind her cabin. Then Reid left her with a quick kiss to her cheek, while she went to the infirmary, tiptoed past a sleeping Sally, and slid into the bed on the other side of the aisle. Still feeling the lingering of that kiss, and everything that had come before it, as she pulled the sheet up over her.

It was dark, and the camp was quiet and asleep. And somewhere out there Reid was sneaking away like a thief in the night. In a sense, though, that's what he was, because he had stolen something from her. Not her virginity, not even her sense of moral purpose. More like her certainty.

With Kevin, there had never been doubts or questions or a roller-coaster of emotion. Their meeting, their dating, their marriage had always been the practical matters she'd wanted them to be.

With Reid there was nothing practical about it. Not one little aspect. That's where her certainty wavered because, for the first time in her life, she wasn't sure she wanted to be all that certain. Wasn't sure she could be any more. And that's what scared her. What truly, honestly scared her.

Raising herself up to peek out the window, Keera saw Reid heading round to the rear side of his cabin and imagined him going in through his kitchen door. An affair with Reid Adams—and, yes, this was an affair of some sort—was like zip lining, where she was flying through the air, tethered to a very small cable. The zip-line cable she trusted because it was proven. Her own private cable wasn't proven, however, which meant disaster could surely be sneaking around in the dark, the way Reid was.

Only this time she wasn't wearing a safety helmet or any of the other protective gear. And she feared that she needed all she could get—to protect her heart.

CHAPTER EIGHT

"IT'S WHERE?" KEERA asked, clearly alarmed by the forest fire that was now engulfing one of the surrounding ridges. She and Reid hadn't had contact for an entire day. In fact, she'd refused to even look at him. But the memories had lingered, made her mellow, caused her to sigh wistfully more times than she wanted to. Nice aftermath with too many warm, leftover sensations. Then this. Life changing too fast, too unpredictably.

"About four miles east of here. I talked to one of the rangers a little while ago, and he wants us to get ready to evacuate. They're hoping that if weather holds, and everything works in their favor, they'll get it contained before it makes it all the way down to this valley. But he also advised that we need to get the kids out of here pretty soon."

"Then that's what we do," she said, seeing the worried look on Reid's face. He had a lot at risk here. Everything he owned, a life's investment in jeopardy. "So, in spite of trying to look calm, I know you're not," she said. "And I think I need to know the worst-case scenario."

"Other than the obvious problems that I may lose my camp, or the smoke that's going to make some of these kids sick, I just went down to the highway, and the roads are already congested. People driving crazy, trying to get out of the valley. I don't want the kids caught up in all that mess."

"Do you have a back-up plan?"

He nodded. "Already implemented. But I'm worried about the time crunch."

However it worked out, it was time to disband camp and in doing that leave all kinds of unresolved feelings behind. Couldn't be helped, though, couldn't be prevented, couldn't even be postponed. Because once she walked away from this place, that's exactly what would happen. Nothing would be resolved, not about her growing feelings for Reid and especially not about what to do with Megan. "How much time do we have?" she asked.

"Not a lot. Maybe an hour, an hour and a half before it starts getting critical. So let me call a staff meeting, get everybody in on this, because we're going to have some disappointed kids. Today was the day we were going to go horseback riding."

"Have you called your partner and told him not to come?"

Reid nodded. "He's my back-up plan. He's up in the sky right now, looking at the fire, assessing our best options. We do mountain search and rescue, so he's authorized to be overhead. And he's ready to come and grab us, depending on the roads."

"Helicopter?" she asked.

Reid nodded.

"Seriously?" The more she heard about Reid's medical practice, the more impressed she was.

Reid grinned. "Which was why I got my pilot's license recently. The chopper is what we make house calls and hospital runs in. Oh, and we go out on horseback for some of the closer house calls. Personally, I prefer my motorcycle over the horse."

* * *

"You're a pilot *and* you have a motorcycle? Let me just say *wow* to your diversity." Keera laughed. "I wouldn't have taken you for a cowboy doctor. But a pilot? I can see that. And I can definitely picture you in leathers. I hope you wear leathers on the motorcycle."

"That would make me some kind of a bad boy, wouldn't it?"

"I saw the bad boy in you last night, Reid. Trust me, the leathers would only enhance what's already there."

Blushing slightly, Reid cleared his throat. "That's me, pilot-cowboy-bad-boy-doctor. But today I'm all camp counselor, who's trying to figure out the most efficient way to get these kids out of here. Which I think will be by air. Also, by taking the kids out in the chopper we can keep them together better until we can make arrangements for their parents to come get them."

"And they'll have a blast doing this, as long as we don't let them know why we're evacuating. You know, turn it into an adventure rather than an emergency." She regarded his brooding expression and her heart went out to him. Sure, she'd spent the night with him. And, sure, she admired him for what he did here. But he was struggling, and so distressed, yet he was trying to hold it all together for everyone else. Who held it together for Reid, though? As far as she knew, nobody.

"The kids are going to be fine, Reid. Trust me, everything's going to turn out OK. They'll be safe, and that's all that matters."

"You're right. That's all that matters." That's what he said, but it's not how he'd sounded when he'd said it.

Keera stepped forward and wrapped her arms around him. "Your camp's going to be safe, isn't it? I mean, it's not in any real danger of…"

She couldn't bring herself to say the words, because she knew how much of Reid's life was tied up in these few wooded acres, and to even think it was at risk made her gut knot.

"The big danger here is the smoke, right? If the wind shifts?" She was saying that to reassure herself, although nothing on Reid's face was reassuring about anything, and she knew what he was thinking, what he was dreading.

"Let's hope so," he said, responding to her embrace by wrapping his arms around her. "But if it burns…well, what I can say?"

"You can say that you took care of the kids first."

"That's right. You're always practical, aren't you?"

"Yep. Always practical." She forced herself out if the embrace. "So now what?"

"Now we get everybody the hell out of Camp Hope."

"Then I'll get the staff together while you figure out what we need to do to get this camp shut down."

"About last night," he started, then stopped when Emmie came running up to him and latched onto his hand.

"When do we get to go riding?" she asked. "Because I told Molly and Nathan I'd show them how because they've never been on a horse before, and I have!"

"Sorry, sweetheart," Reid said. "But we're going to have to save that for another day. Beau can't bring the horses right now."

"But he promised," she whined.

"And we'll do it another time." He looked over at Keera, who was already running in the direction of the dorm. "Today, instead of horseback riding, it's helicopter rides for everyone. So go tell your friends to get ready, that Doc Beau is going to be here with his chopper in a few minutes."

"Really?" Emmie cried. "We're going to fly? You're

not going to say *no* when it's my turn? Because you always say *no* when we're home."

"I'm not going to say *no*. Before long you're going to be going up and over that mountain," he said, pointing to a ridge in the opposite direction from the fire.

"Promise?"

"Cross my heart," he said, crossing his heart as she shooed Emmie back to the other children.

"Everybody's alerted, and getting ready to get out," Keera shouted, running up to him minutes later. "And I was thinking, maybe the kids can all come back later this summer and make up their last couple of days. I know if I can get the time off I'd come back and help you."

He glanced up in the sky, looking for Beau, saw the helicopter off in the distance. "Did you say what I thought you said? That you'd come back?"

"If you needed me to. I mean, I did volunteer for a week, and I'm still good for it."

"I appreciate that, Keera. You don't know how much. And I appreciate everything you've done here so far, even if I've given you a hard time about certain things."

"They're your kids, you have the responsibility."

"And I'm stubborn."

"As stubborn as I am?" she teased.

"Is anybody as stubborn as you are?" When he saw Beau's helicopter making its final approach the somberness slid back down over him. "Guess it's time to get this thing started."

"You don't like the idea of these kids flying, do you?"

"I don't like the idea that this might overstress some of the kids, and I won't be on the other end to take care of them. Because they will hear about the fire. Might even see it from the air."

"I called the sheriff in Marston Springs, Reid. He's

going to be contacting Beau about where to land then he's going to get the doctor over there ready to look at the kids once they set down."

"That's a good instinct," Reid said appreciatively, as the camp staff began to gather around him. "Remind me to invite you back to camp some time."

A minute later all but a couple of people who were busy attending to the kids were huddled around Reid, who was on the phone to the ranger. "Looks like the wind is shifting, and it's coming this way. Not fast, but we're going to start airlifting out of here immediately." He drew in a deep breath.

"You all know the emergency plan. Beau will take charge of getting you on the chopper, Betsy is gathering up the medicines we need to take with us, and Keera has arranged to have the local doc meet us over in Marston Springs. Other than that…" he shrugged "…have a safe trip, and I'll see you on the other side of the mountain.

"Oh, and anybody who wants to drive out is welcome to try. The highway is congested, but if you know your way through Moores Valley, he suggests using the Moores Valley road and taking the turnoff to Marston Springs from that."

As it turned out, only Clara opted to drive, and that was because of her basset hound. The other six volunteers agreed to go by chopper and take care of the kids when they arrived at the other end.

"And Megan?" Keera asked Reid.

"We'll fly her out with the rest of the kids, put her in a chopper with the volunteers to keep them separated. Or you can drive her out. It's up to you."

"What about you?"

"Hanging in to the bitter end. I can't leave until I know everything here is as protected as it can be. And I'm hoping to rescue all the computers. I've got the data backed up to the cloud, but the equipment is expensive and I'd like to save it."

"But you can't stay here by yourself," Keera protested. "It's not safe. What if something happens to you, and you're the only one here? Who's going to help you?"

"Nothing's going to happen to me," he said, taking hold of Keera's hand and heading towards the clinic. "I'll get everybody out, load up what I can, and hang around a day or two to shut the place down if the fire doesn't get it, maybe let parents back in to pick up their kids' things, and hope nothing happens."

"What about your girls?"

"Beau's going to take them back to Sugar Creek with him, and he and Deanna will look after them."

"Will they look after one more?" she asked.

"What do you mean?"

"Megan. Will they look after Megan while I stay here with you?"

"You can't stay! It's not…"

"Safe?"

"It might not be safe. And you're not experienced."

"Does that mean you're experienced with forest fires?" she asked.

"No. Until a few months ago I was a city boy. Only came to the country to be closer to my camp."

"Then shut up and quit arguing with me. If it's safe enough for you to stay behind, it's safe enough for me. I'm not leaving you here alone, and I'm not going to fight you about it."

"But Megan needs a familiar face. She's already gone through enough, and to be put in the arms of strangers again…."

"And she'll have a familiar face in a day or so. Look,

Reid. I've already made up my mind, and there's not a darned thing you can do to stop me, short of tying me up and throwing me on the helicopter." She smiled. "And I'd like to see you try."

"Are you sure about this, Keera? Because if the fire accelerates…"

"Then we'll be in it together." She shrugged. "No big deal. We'll take that back road you suggested."

"It's a very big deal," he said, tilting his head down to give her a gentle but oh-so-brief kiss on the lips. "And I appreciate it. Oh, and so you'll know, you're not the woman I thought you were."

"In a good way or a bad way?"

"Tell you later," he said looking towards the east, as the normal smoke in the mountains, which was actually mist and humidity that lurked just above the treetops, was being engulfed by real and very ominous black smoke. "Because right now I've got to go get the kids ready to ride."

Keera's first instinct was to run to get Megan ready, and when she got to the infirmary Megan was wide awake, looking much better than she had in days. "I don't know what's going to happen after today," she said to Megan as she relieved Sally of duty and helped dress the little girl in street clothes, "but it's not going to be an institution. I can promise you that. Even if you have to come and stay with me for a little while until arrangements can be made."

She glanced wistfully out the window and saw Reid lead a parade of kiddies across the compound. "I'm still not giving up on him, though. I'm just not as optimistic that I have time to convince him to be my solution."

Once Megan was dressed, Keera did a quick exam to make sure she wasn't running a temperature or had some other problem going on, then she bundled her into her arms, carried her outside and fell in line with the rest of the people awaiting their turn for a helicopter ride. The adults were waiting with a sense of trepidation while the kids were anxious and excited. But Reid looked more worried than he had earlier. He kept glancing up at the ridge in the distance, watching the smoke get thicker. And closer.

"Maybe we ought to go, too," she said, sidling up next to him. "Get everybody out of here first then drive out together."

He took Megan from her arms. "It's all I have. All I own. This camp. I've put everything I have into it. And I have to be here, no matter what happens to it."

"But you have your girls, Reid, which makes you a lucky man. The rest…" She looked around, saw the man she assumed to be Beau waving her over. "I think it's time for Megan to fly."

"She'll be fine. Sally's going to hold her, and I'll let Beau know she's to go home with them for the time being."

"By chopper?"

"No. Deanna's driving over to get the girls because Beau's going to hang around and join in rescue efforts."

"But that will expose Emmie to measles."

"Desperate times, desperate measures. If she gets measles, I'll get her through it."

Something about Beau's courage brought tears to her eyes. Or maybe it was the smoke beginning to waft in. She didn't know which it was but she nodded numbly as she watched Reid walk forward to place Megan in Sally's arms. Suddenly a lump the size of her fist formed in her throat and that, added to her already spilling tears, caused her to run forward and take the child from his arms. "I need to do this," she said, sniffling as she carried Megan the rest of the way over. "Look, sweetheart, I'll see you in a little while. I promise. These nice people are going to take you on a ride, and you're going to go stay at a very nice place where they have horses."

"Mommy," she whimpered.

"I know you want her, but Mommy can't be here, sweetheart." Megan hadn't said very much over the past few days—Megan had assumed because of the trauma from her accident combined with being sick—and it was so good to hear her voice. In fact, it caused the lump in her throat to swell a little more. "And we'll talk about that next time I see you. But right now, promise me you'll be good. Can you do that for me?"

Megan nodded, and Keera kissed her on the forehead. Then reluctantly handed her over to Sally, who took her immediately to the helicopter. In another minute they were lifted off the ground and turning away from Camp Hope. And Keera felt so hopeless. Maybe as hopeless as she'd felt all those times when, as a child, her mother had abandoned her. The same way she was sure Megan was feeling right now—abandoned and cast off to strangers.

"They'll be fine," Reid said, as he slipped his arm around her waist. "Deanna's great with kids. So are Brax and Joey…he runs the ranch. They'll take good care of her. And just so you know, I think she was calling *you* Mommy. She's growing attached to you, Keera."

She swiped at her tears. "I hope not, because life's about to jump out and bite her in the ugliest possible way, and…"

"You want to keep her, don't you?"

She shook her head. "I want you to keep her because I can't. She needs a good family now, and you and the girls are the best one I know. You can give her a life that I can't, and she deserves that."

"But it's still not for you—the whole family thing."

"You're right. It's still not for me." For the first time in her life she actually regretted the words. "There are things inside people they can't change, and for me, that's one of them."

"Do you think I ever anticipated being the single father of two little girls?"

"Maybe it's something you didn't anticipate, but you come from a background that doesn't limit you in the capacity it takes to be a father. And not just a father but a good father. I'm limited, Reid. More than you can know. More than I want to know."

"And limits can't be overcome?"

She laughed. "You're always the optimist, aren't you?"

"When it comes to you, yes, I am. Maybe that's because I don't see limits, maybe it's because I see someone fighting hard against so much potential. I still think it's in you, Keera. I'm not sure how to convince you it's there, though."

He couldn't, because it wasn't. But it was so nice to hear him tell her she had potential. No one ever had, not for any reason, and not in any endeavor. Too bad she was hearing about a flat-lined potential that couldn't be shocked back with a defibrillator.

Less than an hour later, after the chopper lifted off for the last time, the camp felt utterly desolate. Reid wasn't sure where Keera was and, right now, standing out here in the compound alone, watching the tail of the helicopter disappear over the ridge, he was spooked. Had to admit it. He was spooked, and it wasn't about being here so much as it was about what he stood to lose if the camp got caught in the fire.

"It's getting closer," Keera called from the porch of the infirmary. She'd been gathering up all the new clothes and toys she'd bought for Megan and packing them into a box to take away with her when she left. "I was looking out the back way, and it's moved down quite a lot. So, what can we do? Should we be hosing down the buildings or something?"

He could feel the grit of the smoke in his lungs now. Or maybe it was his imagination because that's what he expected to feel. Either way, she was right. The fire was marching down the side of the mountain like an invading army, and there wasn't much he could do except put as much gear into the camp van as he could, and keep his fingers crossed.

"If it comes any closer, yes." Who was he kidding? If the fire came any closer it would take the camp with it no matter what they did.

"Is there anything to pack up and take with us?"

"Don't know," he said on a discouraged sigh. "I don't really have much here that's of any value. I've packed all the girls' things, and gone through and gathered everything of value the kids left behind. As far as medical equipment…" He shrugged. "It's insured, and none of it was new to begin with."

"So why stay?"

"Because I'm the captain of this ship. It's all I own. When I decided to do this, I invested everything I had in it. Guess it goes to show you how fragile life is, doesn't it?" He looked up at the fire, which was now visible from their vantage point. A while ago it had only been the smoke threatening Camp Hope, now it was the fire itself.

"But the kids are safe. I talked to Betsy, and they're having fun on their adventure. The Marston Springs sheriff let the kids all ride in his police car, sirens blaring, and now he's treating them to ice cream. The doctor there said every last one of them is fine, and the parents have all been notified and are on their way. Deanna Alexander's already on the way back to Sugar Creek with the girls, so it's a good outcome, Reid. Maybe not the one you wanted, but everybody is safe. So it's time to go."

He looked up into the sky. "Maybe you're right. But damn it all! Why did this have to happen?"

She took hold of Reid's hand and walked with him over to where her car was parked next to the camp van. "Life dealt me a pretty bad hand once so I know what bitterness feels like, and it's not a good feeling because it consumes you, and sucks in everything around you. I understand your bitterness, Reid. But I also understand your strengths, and those strengths will get you through this."

"My girls," he said. "They're my strength."

"The camp is important for them—for Emmie because she's a survivor, and even for Allie because she has a connection to leukemia as a donor that few people ever have. So, if it burns down, you'll build it up again and your girls will be there to help you. It's as simple as that."

"Would that be two or three girls?"

"I shouldn't have said anything. But I thought…"

"You thought one more wouldn't matter."

"That's bad of me, isn't it?"

"Not bad so much as…unfortunate. Because you've got all the qualities. You just don't want to see them."

"My qualities." She laughed bitterly. "Like I told you, my mother was a prostitute, Reid. A prostitute! We lived on the street, half my meals came from whatever I could scrounge from garbage cans, and we were homeless half the time. Or when she did manage a room, she'd put me in the closet while she…she did her thing with the men. Sometimes I lived in cardboard boxes or under bridges, and I hardly ever got to go to school because we never stayed one place long enough.

"Then when I was thirteen, social services finally took me from her, but only because I went to the library every chance I could to read, and confided to my favorite librarian that my mother wanted me to do…do what she did. You know, turn tricks for money because I was developed, and pretty. And young. So I talked to the librarian, who was nice to me, and she helped. If she hadn't, I don't even want to think how it might have turned out.

"But after that, after I was in the system, I was wild, couldn't be controlled, couldn't be kept in a home because I did everything I could to act up. Kind of like my mother was, come to think of it. But I was smart, which is the only saving grace I had in this life because I whizzed through school once I was allowed to go, and even managed to graduate early. Got scholarships, and the rest…" She shrugged.

"The rest isn't fit to be called mother because I'm not going to let anything stand in my way of achieving what I need to achieve. That was the only promise I made to myself through everything, and I've never broken it. I won't let *anything* stand in my way.

"But I know my limitations, and I'm more than ready to admit what I'm not capable of doing. I've been a wife once and failed miserably at that, but Kevin moved on to a life he wanted. A child doesn't have that same option when a parent is bad. I didn't, and I don't want to put another child in the same position I was in. Which is why I'd hoped…"

"Hoped I'd keep Megan."

"So sue me for trying. I don't want bad things for her. In fact, I want only the best."

"Which isn't you?"

"Which isn't me. But I'm good with it."

"I saw how reluctant you were to let Megan go a while ago. That's not being good with it, Keera. If anything, I think you're kidding yourself. And I'm sorry about your childhood. I can't even begin to imagine what it must have been like for you, but you persevered. You got through it and look at you now—what you do, who you are. You're not the little girl who lived in cardboard boxes, and you're not your mother."

"Maybe I'm not but…" Pausing, she smiled. "But I'm me, the person I designed me to be. And I didn't design children into that."

"Then update the design."

"What if I did? What if I *updated* and tried, then somewhere along the way realized that I had been right about it all along? That I wasn't cut out to be a mother? Or, God forbid, that I was like my mother? What would happen to Megan then? I mean, living in a situation where you're not wanted. I don't think you can understand that. It's desolate. There's no hope. And I don't want to do that to her."

"But what if you discovered that you *are* cut out to be a mother? Keera, you're so strong that if you turned out to be like your mother, it would only be by choice. You are who you want to be, and you're completely in control of that, no matter what you might think."

"No matter what I might think? What I think, Reid, is that rolling the dice on who I am is taking a big risk. That's what it would be."

"But if you're capable of designing yourself into the person you want to be, and you want to be a mother, doesn't it stand to reason you can design that into yourself?"

"You've got an argument for everything, don't you?"

"Not everything. But I know I'm right about this. And I do understand how you're afraid you'll turn out to be just like your mother. But, Keera, I can promise you that's never going to happen. You just have to trust yourself more to believe it."

"Most of my life I've tried so hard not to be like her because…"

He took her hand and held it. "Your mother's life was a choice, Keera. Just like your life is a choice. You get to control what you do, what you want, what you want to include. And your mother has no influence in that because you've become your own person.

"I think, though, that you use her as your excuse—to succeed, to excel. You know, be the success you are to prove yourself to the mother who never loved you. The thing is, you can't change what she was. That part of your life is over with, and whatever bad things you were taken away from are in your past.

"Now you don't need to have an excuse to succeed, because all the qualities you'll ever need are in you, totally independent of anything your mother did or was. It's you, Keera. Not her. You can't go back and make her love you, and you're never going to turn into her. So I only hope you'll find a way to trust that and move on. Because until you do, you're depriving yourself of happiness and all the good things you deserve."

"Look, I appreciate what you're trying to do but I really was on the verge of abandoning Megan here a few nights ago and that, if nothing else, should tell you who I am. I didn't want her, and I was angry I had to deal with her. You were her doctor, you ran a camp for kids. I saw you as my solution. And I still do, but differently. And that *is* what my mother would do."

"But it's not what *you* did. That's the difference. She would have, and you didn't. That's all that matters, Keera. You didn't do it."

"That tendency is in me, Reid. Can't you see that? I would have left her here that first night if I'd had the opportunity."

"That tendency is there because you won't let your mother go and, subconsciously, you're sabotaging yourself into thinking you'd be just like her given the opportunity. It's time to quit trying to prove you're not her and start trying to prove you're you. But I can't be the one to convince you of that. It has to be you."

"I appreciate your faith in me, as misplaced as it is."

He'd give her credit for one thing. She was as stubborn as hell, and he didn't know what it was going to take to crack that shell of hers so she could see what was inside. Truth was, she was afraid to look, afraid of what she might find. Even though he understood why, he still couldn't understand why she refused to take that hard, objective look and see all the things he saw. Especially when, just a little while ago, she'd actually gone teary over putting Megan on the helicopter.

Well, at least he saw the conflicts for what they were. What he couldn't see, though, was the reason for his own emotional entanglement. He knew who Keera was and what she resisted, which was essentially everything he wanted in life. Yet he was fascinated. More than fascinated, actually. He was downright captivated, and he didn't know how to undo that. But he had to. That's all there was to it. He had to.

CHAPTER NINE

IT WAS TIME to get out, but Reid was still working methodically, trying to pack away as much as he could in the camp van. Just working. Not talking. And not looking at the fire creeping its way across the valley the way she was drawn to looking. Because he didn't want to see his future. Much the way she didn't want to see various aspects of her own life. Some things were too painful to face—for both of them.

"Anything else I should get?" she asked him. "I've got a little more room for a few small things." Her eyes stung, her throat ached. Her lungs were fighting for every breath now. But she wasn't going to leave him here alone.

Pausing in his frantic efforts, he wiped the sweat from his face with the back of his hand, then shook his head. "I've done all I can. It's time to go. You lead, I'll follow. We'll stick to the highway unless it's too congested, then I'll call you."

"When it's over, Reid, no matter how it goes, maybe I can help you get the camp up and running again. Not so much in the physical sense but I've got some contacts, people who might be able to take on some of the responsibility." She smiled. "I've operated on some people in mighty high places, so all I have to do is call."

"You'd do that?" he asked, walking her to her car. "Stay

involved here past, well…past all this?" For the first time since the kids had all gone he looked across the valley at the fire, saw how close it was to the east end of his acreage.

"I would," she said.

"Why? Why would you be willing to help me when…?"

"When I don't like kids?"

"That's not what I was going to say, but it is a good question as you're not fond of them."

"See, that's the thing. I'm not *not* fond of children. In fact, I've enjoyed my association with Megan, and even with your girls. But I lack that elusive thing some people call the parenting gene, so I'm not a nurturer by nature. Which doesn't mean I'm a kid-hater. More like an avoider.

"But this camp, Reid, it's so important. I know what we did, what we had was only a one-night thing, and I'm not kidding myself about that. It was good. Fantastic. But it was last night, and today I'm extending my hand in friendship because you're going to need help with something that's worthy. Whether or not you accept it is entirely up to you, but the offer stands.

"I'll help do whatever needs to be done when the time comes, if you want me to. Or stay away, if that's what you want. But right now let's just get out of here."

"Agreed," he said, as he opened her door for her. "And I'll see you on the other side of the mountain. Oh, and…" He bent down, gave her a quick kiss on the lips. "Thank you," he whispered. "For everything."

"Be safe, Reid," she said, as she moved her car forward. "Please be safe," she whispered to herself as she looked in her rear-view mirror and saw him climb into his van. "So we can meet on the other side of the mountain."

She wouldn't see what he'd done. And by the time she'd figured out that he'd turned off onto an access road at the edge of the property, she'd be safe in Marston Springs. And he'd be attempting one last-ditch effort, by moving all the volunteers' cars as far away from the camp enclosure as possible then hosing down the buildings. It wouldn't be easy, probably wouldn't even be successful, but he couldn't go down without this fight. And he couldn't have fought knowing someone he loved was in the path of danger.

She wasn't, though. Not now. So parking his van a good distance from the compound, he got out and went, on foot, back to the area, where he started, one by one, to move the cars away. Potential gasoline explosions and all. Although there weren't any good places to stash them, he did take them to a cleared area on the west side of the property— a baseball field. The first car, then second one. Driving frantically, wishing he didn't have to waste the time, wishing he could have had his volunteers do this, but knowing they'd had to take care of the children instead.

Still, getting rid of the explosion hazard made him feel like he was doing something, even if it was futile, and as he ran back that nearly quarter-mile to get the next car, he saw a vehicle approaching him. "What the…?"

"I saw the keys in the cars," she shouted out the window at him. "Figured out you'd want these cars moved at some point if you were going to fight it. Then when I saw you turn off on the access road…"

"You saw that?"

"I'm a surgeon. I observe everything."

"You can't do this. Can't be here."

"But you are."

"Seriously? You're going to get stubborn with me now?"

Rather than answering, she rolled up her car window and continued down the road, while he was left to run back and bring yet another car up. Which was when he met her on the road and stopped. "I'll be fine here. You don't need to do this because…"

"Because I want to? Look, Reid. My life doesn't count for much outside the operating room, but this camp, it adds something and, like you, I'm not going to let it go up in flames without a fight. So…" She gave a shooing gesture then spun away and continued her run down the road to fetch the next car. And so it went until all the cars were cleared away.

"Bet we're not leaving yet, are we?" she asked him when they were both finally back at the compound, running hand in hand.

What they found was not promising. The fire had encroached by jumping the dirt road on the east, and was spreading quickly along the fire trail all the way up to the compound itself—in patchy splotches, though. Thankfully not one great consuming wall of fire. Right now advance small fires were burring rather lazily, like they were waiting for the rest to catch up to them. But they were shooting off blazing embers, one after another. Little bursts of fireworks that would have been lovely in a holiday celebration but so deadly here, and now.

"I'll get the hose," Keera said, as Reid went in the opposite direction to grab a shovel.

When she returned with the hose, she saw him smashing the little blazers down as they hit the dirt, ignited the flower garden and a couple of wooden chair sitting on the edge of the compound. Then the tool shed. That's where Keera went into action, turning on the water and dousing the little wooden structure as best she could.

She had success, initially. The roof suffered damage, but the fire went out without much of a protest and it was a good thing because one of the outlying, unused cabins took an ember to the roof, which quickly had the whole roof flaming, taunting her to come get it, too. Which she did, or tried to. But by the time she dragged the hose over the ground and got it aimed, the roof was already half-gone, which meant the cabin itself wouldn't be long in following.

"Reid," she shouted, looking overhead as another burning ember floated merrily on its way, headed towards her cabin! "I can't contain it here."

"Get back!" he shouted, as his attention caught on the same ember that had caught hers. "Let it burn, and stay away."

Not to be deterred by the embers, she did let that cabin go and immediately ran to her own cabin and started to douse at almost the same time as the roof started to blaze. But her position wasn't good enough and the pine tree that loomed above it caught fire, too, and exploded into flames quicker than anything she'd ever seen burn. Another loss, only this one she fought valiantly, alternately spraying the walls and roof of the cabin as best she could.

The problem was the fiery tree above it had spread the flames to the next tree over, then the one after that, and that's when Keera realized that every last one of the guest cabins in that row would fall victim.

After that she looked around, saw Reid still beating out the small ground fires, which were overtaking him now. Saw that the next structure to go, after the guest cabins, would be the dorm, where the children stayed. And the one after that the dining hall.

"We can't save it," she said, wiping sooty sweat from her brow. It was a realization she hated with everything in her. But it was a fact. The fire had encroached enough that everything on the outer sides of the compound would go up. The dorms, Reid's cabin. Maybe not the clinic, though, which sat in the open and isolated from everything else.

"Reid," she yelled. "All of this." She shook her head. "We can't save it. But your clinic…"

"No! This time we've got to get out of here for real," he shouted back. "It doesn't make a difference now."

"But it does, if we can save that one thing."

"We've got to leave," he said, running up to her. "Before we get trapped."

"But the clinic!"

"Keera, it's only a building. A stupid, damned building." He grabbed the hose away from her, turned off the nozzle, and dropped it to the ground. "It doesn't matter any more. It's all…done."

"But the clinic, that's where you can start over, if we save it. And I want to try, Reid. Please, let me try."

He grabbed hold of her to tug her away from the compound but she resisted and pulled back. "You don't understand," she cried. "You have to fight for the things you love, the things you want in your life. If you don't…"

"I'm fighting for you, Keera, not for the clinic. It's time to go."

She shook her head. Bent down and picked up the hose. "No," she choked, as sooty tears rolled down her cheeks. "We have to try."

"Is this because if I lose everything I won't adopt Megan as I'll be too involved in trying to start over?"

"Wh-what? How could you even think that?"

"What am I supposed to think? That you've had a change of heart, fallen in love with me, even though I have kids? That you want to do this because you want to build a life around me, my children, and even this?"

"Reid, that's not fair!"

"Isn't it? I'm about to lose a large part of my dream, and here you are, fighting harder than I am to hang onto it. Which doesn't make any sense. So why wouldn't I think you're doing this because it's about you? You've never shown me anything that would make me think otherwise!"

This couldn't be happening. He couldn't be saying these things to her. "You don't mean it," she said. "You're talking crazy because the camp is burning down."

"It's not crazy talk, Keera. It's what I think."

"Then you think wrong." She turned and started to walk away. Then spun back to face him. "To hell with you, Reid Adams. To hell with this camp, to hell with your life." They were words that broke her heart because all she'd wanted to do was save a little piece of his dream for him—his starting point for rebuilding that dream.

"Oh, and if you're afraid that now's when I walk away and abandon Megan with you, to hell with you on that one, too."

Keera didn't turn round again. Not to see the expression on his face, not to watch him follow her. No, she went straight to her car, got in and didn't look back. Not when she fetched Megan in Marston Springs and dropped off the camp belongings with Betsy, not when she headed for the highway that took her home. And not even when she had to pull off the highway and have the hardest cry of her life.

"What have I done?" she asked herself in the mirror as muddy tears streaked down her cheek.

The toddler sleeping in her car seat didn't answer. Neither did the reflection in the mirror. Only her heart did, and it wasn't telling her what she wanted to hear.

"OK, let's get you ready to go to daycare," Keera said, as she looked at the mess of toys spread from one wall to the other. Her guest room, now a temporary nursery, looked like a tornado had hit it. So maybe she wasn't the tidiest temporary mom. Her once-weekly housekeeper picked up every Friday, which gave Keera and Megan a fresh start on a new week of messiness. Four weeks in a row now had turned it into a workable routine. Scatter for six days, pick up on the seventh.

And thank heavens for the hospital daycare center. That alleviated her problems in ways she'd never anticipated. They were open seven days, twenty-four hours, and the care was excellent. She knew, because that's where she took her breaks now, instead of hiding away in her office to review a patient history or grab a thirty-minute nap. Now her breaks were spent coloring or finger-painting or sharing graham crackers and milk with Megan. Something she actually enjoyed.

What she didn't enjoy, though, was being alone, having no one there to tell her if she was doing the mothering thing the right or wrong way. She had no instinct for it, but common sense seemed to be working out pretty well. And social services were still looking for an adoptive family. Although Keera wasn't pressing them now.

In fact, she'd told the social worker she'd like to keep Megan for a while longer, and she'd even gone to the effort of starting to legalize her guardianship. Why? For Megan's security, above all. Megan needed this time to adjust. She knew her real mommy and daddy weren't coming back, and she'd become so clingy with Keera that Keera didn't have the heart to send her away until she was more ready than she was now.

But also Reid had been right. She'd thought about his words, over and over, and had eventually come to realize how she'd spent a lifetime trying to prove she wasn't her mother, trying to do exactly the opposite of what her mother had done. Yet in her own heart she'd never truly discovered what she would do without that motivation.

What she would do, though, was love taking care of Megan. Which she did. And which was why, while she still wanted the best adoptive situation for her, there wasn't such an urgency about it now. At some point the time would come to give her up. Keera knew that, rationalized it every single day. Even dreaded it. And when that time came Keera knew her heart would break.

But this was all about Megan now, and what was best for her. Still, for now, every day was a new and better step. And who knew what would happen in the future? For sure, she didn't.

So even though everything was up in the air, Keera was happier than she could remember being. But she missed Reid. Missed him desperately. Unfortunately, that was a bridge that had burned down with his camp.

The newspaper and Internet had carried accounts of the camp's destruction. Nothing specific, only that it was closed down now and that the owner was making no comment about its future. No injuries had been reported from the camp, none from the forest fire either. It had started with a campfire in an unauthorized area. One single, lousy campfire and she'd lost countless hours sleep because she missed Reid, missed the camp, missed his daughters, missed all the things she hadn't known she'd wanted until it was too late.

"After work, we're going to go do some shopping, maybe buy a pizza for dinner," she told Megan. She was surprised a child so young would love pizza the way Megan did, but the child begged for it practically every day. "And tomorrow, when I'm not working—" and blessedly not on call "—we'll go to the zoo. You'll get to see lions and elephants and zebras. Do you know what a zebra is, Megan?"

"No," the girl said.

"Then after you're dressed, how about we find a picture on the Internet?"

"Is it purple?" she asked. Like she'd discovered Megan's favorite food was pizza, she'd also discovered her favorite color, and had even had a decorator come in and redo the guest room in little-girl decor, predominantly purple.

"No, sweetie. It's black and white, with crazy stripes."

"Crazy stripes," Megan parroted.

"A whole bunch of them." She helped Megan put on her own socks then put on her shoes and tied them. Purple shoes, pink socks. Pink was a definite concession in a purple girl's life. The thing was it was amazing to see how many opinions Megan had. Until she'd brought her home, Keera had had no clue a child so young had preferences and opinions, and, boy, had she been wrong about that.

Little Miss Megan, once she became comfortable in her new surroundings, was all opinion and preference. So much so that in an adult it might have been annoying. But in a two-year-old it was as cute as could be. Which officially put her in the category of moms prejudiced by the cuteness of their children—to the point of near-blindness.

But that was OK. This new life was agreeing with her.

What wasn't agreeing with her, though, were her feelings for Reid. They hadn't talked since that day, which was kind of surprising. In fact, for the first week she'd answered her phone with lightning speed, expecting him to call. The second week—not so much. And now, unless it was work related she didn't bother picking up because another call that wasn't him only punctuated how much she missed him. "I'd have thought he would have called to see if we made it home safely."

The timeline for that call was well past now. And she knew it, felt it in her heart and in the pit of her stomach. She'd made her impression, the one she'd intended to make, and was now suffering the consequences. Her fault entirely, and she didn't blame him for that. Only she wished she'd had time to change his mind.

Now he was back in his practice and picking up what was left over from his dream, and she wasn't part of that. And she couldn't be because he didn't want her. Had declined her phone calls the first few days after their break-up.

Break-up? From what? One night together and a whole bunch of conflicting feelings? How could they have broken up when they'd had nothing to break up from?

"Then after the zoo, maybe we'll go to the bookstore as you don't have enough books, and all little girls need lots and lots of books and bedtime stories." To tell the truth, Keera was looking forward to the bedtime stories maybe even more than Megan was. That's what surprised her. As she settled in with the child, it was like she was experiencing childhood again, a better childhood. The childhood she would have liked for herself.

And somewhere, an hour away, Reid was doing the same with his daughters. In a way it was comforting, knowing they were sharing the same experience under the same sky. But in an even bigger way it was heartbreaking because she'd gone and done the one thing she'd vowed never to do. She'd fallen in love. Only not the way she'd fallen in love the first time. This time it was different. Real. Everything. And everything she couldn't have.

"These are the clothes you're going to have to wear. I'm sorry you lost everything you bought with Keera, but I left them behind and saved the computers instead." He knew, for sure, that he couldn't duplicate Keera's effort, not in clothes, not in the girls' sentiments, and he felt bad about that.

Felt bad about a lot of things, like how Emmie and

Allie had begged for weeks to have her take them shopping again. Once he'd almost given in and called her. But one call and he'd lose his resolve. And Keera Murphy wasn't the kind of woman he wanted around his daughters because they got attached, and Keera was incapable of attaching back.

Sadly, he'd gotten himself pretty attached as well. And while there was a part of him that wanted to believe her efforts to save his camp had been genuine, how could he truly believe that when she'd expressed her sentiment clearly, over and over? She didn't want children, and she did want him to adopt the one she had.

"But for now you're going to have to make do."

"But, Daddy," Emmie whined.

He shook his head. "You know what I told you. That for a little while we've got to watch our money. I've got a lot of expenses ahead, and I can't afford…"

Who was he kidding? What he couldn't afford was to have his heart ripped all the way through. It was hanging in tatters as it was. Seeing Keera again would only finish the job. "Work with me here, OK? As soon as I get some of the mess at Camp Hope sorted out, we'll have a shopping day and you can buy whatever you want. But that's going to have to wait for a few weeks." Until he had more time, more energy, more hope.

It was hard hanging on, not just for him but for the girls. Especially when all he owned was some charred acreage and a few remains of buildings. And who would have known there was so much to do in the aftermath of a disaster? Insurance claims, getting the unsafe structures leveled, permits for the work, planners and architects for the camp's future.

During the day, when he was busy, he was optimistic. But the nights were what got to him, when memories of that one perfect night with Keera crept back in spite of his best efforts to keep them out. Then from there, the losses. Too much, too many. He couldn't sleep. Couldn't let the girls see how much he was struggling because they depended on him to be strong. To be Daddy.

"How about a date tomorrow? We'll have ice cream, maybe go to the park or see a movie? How does that sound?"

"OK," Emmie said, her voice definitely lacking enthusiasm.

"OK," Allie mimicked, in the same voice.

One thing was sure, next time a woman walked into his life he wasn't going to bring her around the girls for any reason until everything in the relationship was sorted out and there was a future involved. Because the girls missed Keera, talked about her every day, begged him to get her back.

Something he couldn't do. But something he would if he could. And wanted to so badly.

CHAPTER TEN

"Last night, Daddy," Allie said, her eyes filling with tears. "She didn't want me to tell you. Made me promise, cross my heart."

Reid placed his hand on Emmie's forehead. She was burning up. Practically incoherent. Pale. Sweating. He'd seen this before, last time… Except she was having associated abdominal pain now. So maybe it wasn't another flare-up of leukemia. "That's OK, sweetheart. You're not in trouble."

"Is Emmie sick again?" Allie's bottom lip trembled. "Like last time?"

"She's sick, but not like last time," he said, trying to sound upbeat for both his girls' sakes. Truth was, he didn't know. He hoped, and his objectivity as a doctor told him the symptoms didn't quite match. But as a father, all his worst fears were pummeling him.

"Is it back, Daddy?" Emmie managed to ask. "Did my leukemia come back again?"

"It might be something you ate, as your belly hurts." Or appendicitis. Yes, that's what it was. Appendicitis, which opened up a whole new set of worries, because a quick appendectomy was complicated in the aftermath of leukemia. "I think, though, we're going to have to take you to the hospital and have some tests run to see what it is."

He turned to Beau Alexander, who was already on the phone to the hospital. "If you don't mind, I'd like Joey to fly me. Don't want to waste time in the car."

"He's already fueling up the chopper," Beau said, squeezing his partner on the shoulder.

"Oh, and I have a surgeon on standby, just in case. She's not a general surgeon, but she's agreed to step in and offer an opinion, and she's getting the best general surgeon she knows rounded up, in case we need to go that route."

"Which hospital?"

"Not Mercy. And before you argue with me that you'd feel more comfortable taking Emmie where she's gone before, let me say that you've been moping around here for the past month, and all I've heard is how great Keera is, what a good doctor, good surgeon she is. So I called her, and she's taking care of getting everything ready to receive Emmie at Central Valley. By air, it's only fifteen minutes longer, and I think that right now you're going to need her support."

"And we'll watch Allie, of course. For as long as this takes," Deanna, his wife volunteered.

"I'll step up, too," Brax Alexander, the patriarch of the Alexander family, said. "Can't claim to be a pediatrician but I have my way with the kiddies, so I'll take on your cases until you're ready to get back to work. So there's nothing to worry about here, son. We've got you covered."

Reid let out a huge sigh of relief. He hadn't only become part of a medical practice here in Sugar Creek. He'd become part of a family. "I really appreciate everything."

"You just get that little girl all better and get her back to us as fast as you can," Brax said.

"And patch it up with Keera," Beau said, sliding his arm around his wife's waist. "It's time for you to be happy."

But with Keera? "We'll see," he said as he gave Allie

a kiss, then scooped Emmie into his arms and headed to the front door. Truth was, there wasn't much to be happy about and he wasn't sure he could even fake it, not now that Emmie was sick. If it was leukemia again he'd have to find a way to be strong. If it was appendicitis then maybe having Keera there, making the arrangements, would help. He didn't know. Just didn't know.

The trip was far faster than he'd expected, and he never set Emmie down the whole way. No, he held on to her for dear life, and when Joey landed the helicopter on the hospital's helipad, and when an army of medics rushed and took Emmie away from him, he couldn't think of a time when he'd felt more desolate.

"They'll take good care of her," Keera said, stepping up behind him as the chopper lifted skywards and headed back to Sugar Creek. "I got Wade Andrews, head of oncology and our leukemia specialist, to take charge of her team, and lined up Annabelle Gentry, the best general surgeon I know, in case it's her appendix. Oh, and Brett Hollingsworth, head of Pediatrics, is on his way in to oversee her general care while she's here. I've got her set up in a private room in Pediatrics, and had a bed brought in for you so you can stay."

"I don't know what to say, Keera."

"You don't have to say anything. This is about Emmie, and you know how I feel about her and Allie."

"They've missed you," he said, as she slipped her hand into his and pulled him towards the hospital door.

"I've missed them. You don't know how much I enjoyed our girls' day out. It was a first for me, and it made me realize how much I missed when I was that age. Also how much I like…" she smiled "…being around children."

"See, I told you so."

"Yes, you did, and we'll talk about that later on. Right now, though, tell me about Emmie."

"I didn't know she was sick. Apparently she hasn't felt well for a couple of days—general malaise, vomiting, which she never told me about, achiness, tender belly, feverish. Allie knew, but the girls conspired to keep it a secret because they were afraid if they told me, that would make it be leukemia again."

"We all have ways of deluding ourselves, don't we? Even when we're young, I suppose. Oh, and Allie called me a little while ago."

"Allie?"

"Yep, Allie. She didn't want to talk to you because she was afraid it would make you sad, so she called me. Had Brax dial for her."

"He's a pushover when it comes to kids. Can't ever say no to them."

"Well, he didn't say no to Allie and, Reid, what she said was so sweet. She told me if Emmie is sick like she was before, she wants to be the donor. Actually, she called it a door—near, but I knew what she meant."

"I—I… Twice in a row, I don't know what to say."

"You don't have to. I'll say it for you. You're an amazing father, and you've taught your daughters to be generous." As they stepped into the hospital, they headed straight to Pediatrics, where the team Keera had assembled was fast-working on Emmie. Blood was being drawn, X-rays being taken. Pokes, prods, IV, oxygen, all the usual.

"We're going to get her through this. Whatever it is, I promise, we're going to get her, get both of you, through this."

Reid swallowed hard, looking through the window of the procedure room. "The camp burned to the ground," he said.

"I know. I read the accounts. I'm so sorry."

"Emmie's been helping me with the plans to rebuild. I think I may have a budding architect, because the architect I've hired is actually going to incorporate some of her ideas. He said a kids' camp from a kid's perspective is what I need, and he told her that when she grows up to keep him in mind when she's looking for a…" He slapped a tear from his cheek. "I feel so damned helpless. Done this twice before, I don't know if I can do it again."

Keera stepped up behind him and slid her arm around his waist. "We may not have worked out as a couple, Reid, but I'm your friend, and I'm not going to let you go through this alone. Whatever you and Emmie need, whenever you need it, you don't even have to ask."

"I know," he said. "And I'm sorry. You don't know how much I wanted to answer your calls or call you. Or just come here and see you. Every day, Keera. Every single day of every single week since that day when you walked away from me."

"You were right, though. I didn't give you anything to trust. I was adamant about who I was and what I wanted, and there was no room inside that for us. But it did hurt, Reid, hearing how you believed that my wanting to help you with the camp was me trying to manipulate you. You had a right to that opinion, and everything I'd said or done was responsible for that opinion, and I wasn't even angry at you. It hurt, but I understood."

"Dr. Adams," Dr. Hollingsworth said, stepping out into the hall. "Emmie's pretty sick, but we're not sure yet what's causing it. We've got the first round of tests started, and what I'm proposing, because of her past history, is that we put her in the ICU for close observation until we start getting things sorted out. Might be for a few hours, might be for a few days, until we have everything worked up."

"You don't think she needs her appendix out?"

"There's a possibility but, given her history, we're reluctant to look at that as our first course of action as she's got several swollen lymph glands."

Reid nodded. "I did notice that when I examined her, which is why my first thought was…"

"A recurrence of her leukemia," Dr. Hollingsworth said. "And if Emmie was mine, I'd be thinking the same thing. But Keera said she's been active, not feeling bad."

"I asked Beau when he called me earlier," Keera explained.

"That's right. She was fine. A little tired the past couple of days but before that she was energetic as all get-out."

"In my experience, leukemia doesn't just take you down from being healthy and active one minute to where she is now. So, while we're not going to rule it out, we are looking for other causes. And make no mistake, she's a very sick little girl. But we're optimistic. In the meantime, it's going to take us about an hour to get her transferred to her ICU bed, so the doctors' lounge is available if you'd like to go and wait. And our cafeteria is open around the clock in case you want to grab something to eat. I'll page Keera as soon as we get Emmie situated, then you can come and see her."

"I appreciate it," Reid said, extending his hand to the man.

"Oh, and that camp of yours. I've heard good things. Hope you can get it up and running again because I have a couple of patients who could benefit, and I could be up for a little volunteering myself."

"Working on it," Reid said numbly, because numb was all he felt. Numb, but not alone.

"Are you sure I can't get you something?" Keera asked as they shut the door to the private room that would be Emmie's once she was out of Intensive Care. "Coffee, tea, a soft drink?"

She felt totally helpless because there truly was nothing she could do to help him except stay with him. And that wasn't helping, at least not in the way he needed.

"Thanks, but I'm good."

"You're going to have to keep yourself going for Emmie's sake. You know that, don't you?"

"Is this my pep talk?" he snapped.

"No, it's your reality check. I know you're scared, and I wish I knew what to do to make that better for you but other than being here, trying to take care of you, I can't."

"That's right. Keera the nurturer."

"That's not fair, Reid. And I know you're snapping at me because of Emmie. But I always knew my limitations, and was honest about them. So, please, don't take it out on me now, because I do want to help you."

"I know," he said, sitting down on the side of the guest bed. "And I'm sorry. It's been a horrible few weeks, thinking about everything I did wrong. Then with all the arrangements concerning the camp...now this." He looked up at her. "You didn't deserve what I said about you that day, and you don't deserve it now. I am sorry, Keera. Truly, sorry. Please, believe that."

"I do," she said gently. Then chuckled. "Oil and water. That's us, isn't it?"

He patted the bed, inviting her to sit down next to him. When she did, he pulled her into his arms and simply held her. "Not really. I seem to recall a pretty good mixing."

"We were good, weren't we? And in more ways than *that*."

"In more ways than *that*. But *that* was pretty spectacular."

"Look, Reid. When this is over, when Emmie's back

on her feet and all cured of whatever it is she's caught, and I'm going to believe she caught a bug of some kind until someone tells me otherwise, well, anyway, when it's over, I really do want to help get the camp going again. I've been thinking about it for weeks, wondering what I could do that wouldn't pit us against each other, for starters. So I've decided to rebuild the clinic for you, if you'll let me. Make it a real clinic, though. Not just a make-do cabin. Furnish it with everything you need rather than all the odds and ends, like you had. Will you let me do that for you?"

"Insurance money isn't stretching far enough to get me everything I need. I was on the verge of committing to another make-do clinic simply to get it up and running."

"But I want to do better for the kids." She pulled away from him and looked straight into his eyes. "And I'd like to help with the actual building, as in setting up the interior, if you'll let me. But if you don't think we can work together again, I'll write you a check for whatever you need."

"That's generous. For the third time tonight I don't know what to say."

"Say yes. It's a simple word, and the beginning of something that will be so good."

"The thing is, if Emmie's leukemia has come back, I don't know if I can go through with plans to rebuild. Not now, anyway. Maybe not for a long time to come."

"Then let me take over. You take care of Emmie, and I'll make sure your camp plans go forward."

"Why do you want to do this?" he asked. "Especially after the way I treated you last time you made the offer to help."

"Because I believe now. Believe better, believe differently. And it's also because—" Her cellphone interrupted her, and five seconds later she jumped up from the side of the bed. "Got to leave for a couple of minutes. Be right back."

It was time to visit Megan. She was going through one of her sullen periods, which happened when she missed Keera. And only Keera could take care of fixing it.

"I'm here, sweetheart," she said, picking up the girl, who instantly clung to Keera for dear life.

"She has a real attachment thing going," Dolores, the daycare worker, said. "Kept telling me she wanted her mommy."

"I know she does." But there was no mommy to be had.

"That's you, Doctor. You're mommy to her, no matter what the circumstances. You're the one she wants now."

Keera smiled, not sure what to do. Her initial fears of not being able to manage this were gone. So were her fears about her lack of natural instinct, because she did have her common sense intact. And as far as Megan being Kevin's child, it didn't matter any more. He'd done a good thing bringing this child into the world, and she wasn't a reminder of anything except she was a little girl who needed a real mommy or daddy. "Look, I'm going to keep her with me for a little while. When she gets over this, I may bring her back."

Or she might just beg off the surgical rotation for the morning—she only had one minor procedure scheduled—and ask one of her associates to take it. Then she could stay with Reid and keep Megan comforted as well. For someone who wasn't a nurturer, she seemed to being doing an awful lot of that lately. "I'll call you or whoever's on duty later on and let you know what we're going to do. And in the meantime, I think Miss Megan and I might go down to the cafeteria and find us a banana and yogurt for breakfast. Does that sound yummy to you, Megan?"

With her head tucked as tight as it could be into Keera's

chest, Megan gave her a nod. "Then afterwards we're going to go visit Doc Reid. Do you remember him? He's the nice man who took care of you when you had measles."

She nodded again.

"Oh, by the way," Dolores said as Keera left. "Social services called here yesterday, looking for you. I didn't take the call but I saw the note and wasn't sure if the message got to you or not."

"It didn't," she said, as a lump formed in her stomach, realizing the very best news for Megan could be the very worst news for her.

"Well, you're supposed to call your caseworker as soon as you can. She said it's important but not urgent."

Keera nodded reluctantly, now facing a reality she wasn't sure she wanted to face. "Later. If she calls back, tell her I've got a crisis here at the hospital but I'll get back to her later."

After a quick trip to the cafeteria, then with yogurt, milk, a banana, and a couple of coffees in hand, not to mention a toddler, Keera hurried back up to Reid's room, stopped in her progress by Brett Hollingsworth, who asked her to tell Reid that Emmie was being moved to the ICU right then.

"You've sure turned…well, I guess the only way to describe it is domestic. Just look at you, here in Pediatrics with your child, comforting a worried father, taking on the role of camp counselor."

"Wrong on all counts but one. I am comforting a worried father, because he's my friend. There's nothing domestic involved in that."

"I've heard rumors coming from daycare that you try to get down there to group-sing every day." He grinned. "You know, 'The wheels on the bus go round…'"

"Yeah, yeah," Keera said, shoving past him and hurrying on to the room.

"I'm just saying," Brett called after her.

She ignored him as she pushed open the door, scooted Megan in first, then followed.

"What's this?" Reid asked.

"It's what I do in my spare time now."

"You kept her?"

"Temporarily, which I think may be coming to an end shortly. I mean, when she was sick I promised her I wouldn't let them take her to one of *those* places, and I meant it. I was there, raised in them, and there's no way they're going to do that to her. So I've been managing."

"I'm not surprised," he said, rushing over to take the food and coffee from her. "It's what I saw in you all along."

"No, you didn't. You wanted to, but it wasn't there."

"Yet look at you now."

"Someone else just said that to me," she said, pulling the bedside tray away from the wall and pushing it over to one of the chairs. "And I told him he was wrong." But not as wrong as he once might have been.

"See, there you go again."

She shrugged. "OK, so maybe I'm not as bad at this as I thought I'd be. But I'm still a darned sight further away from parent of the year than you are. Speaking of which, Emmie's being transferred right now, and they should be coming to get you in the next few minutes, once she's settled in."

"You're efficient, Keera."

"Words to turn a girl's heart."

He laughed. "What if I also told you that efficient is sexy?"

"Then I'd nominate you for man of the year." She opened the carton of yogurt and handed a plastic spoon to Megan, who dug right in. "Because most men have other standards for sexy, if you know what I mean. So it's nice to hear that something substantial like being efficient can also be sexy."

"Oh, don't get me wrong. I have the same standards as other men, as far as sexy goes. And you've got all that. But you've got more."

She laughed. "See, now the truth comes out."

A knock on the door startled them both, and a nurse poked her head in the door to tell Reid that he could see Emmie now.

"Give her a hug for me," Keera said, "and tell her I'll come by to see her later on."

"Ten minutes every hour," the nurse warned Reid, as he headed for the door. "Wish we could do better as you're a pediatrician, but I can't. Sorry."

"Then I'll see you back here in twelve minutes," Keera said, and turned her attention to breaking the banana into bite-sized pieces for Megan. Then she dialed the dreaded phone number.

"Hi, Consuela," she said, when the woman on the other end picked up. "It's Keera Murphy, and I understand you've been trying to get a hold of me."

"Hello," Reid said very quietly, as he stood over Emmie's bed and looked down. Even though it was a pediatric ward, she looked so dwarfed—by the bed, by the equipment. It was something he remembered from last time, staring at all the hugeness surrounding his little girl. In ways only a parent could understand, it intimidated him, scared him to death. But he couldn't let on—for Emmie's sake, even for his own.

"Did it come back, Daddy?" she asked weakly.

"We don't know anything yet. But soon, I promise."

"I'm so tired."

"I know you are, which is why you're in here. So you can sleep. That's the only thing you have to do now. Just sleep."

"What about your patients? Who's going to take care of them?"

"That's not for you to worry about," he said, pushing the hair from her eyes. "It's all taken care of. Brax is going to see my patients, and Beau and Deanna are watching Allie, so there's nothing to be concerned about."

"Can I see Keera? I want to tell her how all those clothes we bought got burned up. Do you think she'll take me shopping again?"

"Keera's taking care of Megan right now, but she said she'd come and see you soon. Why don't you ask her yourself if you can go shopping? I think she might..." He didn't finish his sentence. Didn't have to, as Emmie had fallen back to sleep.

"How is she?" Keera asked.

"Worried that all those clothes you bought her got burned up. She wants to go shopping again."

"And I'd love to take her again. Her and Allie, and..." She paused. Frowned.

"What's the matter?"

"I got a call from Megan's social worker," she whispered, so Megan wouldn't hear. "They've found a couple who might want to adopt her. She wants to schedule a first meeting between Megan and them."

"That's good, isn't it?"

She shrugged. "It's what I wanted, initially. No, actually, what I wanted was for you to adopt her. I told you that."

"But it didn't work out."

"And now…" Tears suddenly filled her eyes. "Now it's too late."

"But she'll have a permanent home, Keera. That's what's best for her. And I'm sure the social worker was very choosy in picking out the right parents."

"She does need parents, doesn't she?"

"Or parent. Single parenting has its rewards. If you want to keep her."

"I want to do what's best for her, and I've always known it was a home better than the one I could give her."

"Yet look at her. She's eating, perfectly contented to do it by herself. And she seems to be gaining some independence…some of your independence. That's good mothering, Keera, no matter what you want to call it. You're teaching her what she needs to know, pointing her in the direction she needs to go, and at the end of the day that's all a parent can really do besides love and protect them. So, what else did Consuela have to say?"

"I have to let her know by noon."

"That?"

"That I want to keep her myself—*if* I want to keep her."

"Are you thinking about it?"

"I don't know. Maybe. But I'm so confused. Because getting what I wanted—a home for Megan—doesn't feel as good as it should. It doesn't feel good at all."

"So, let me ask you this. Does Megan make your life better?"

"I know my life is different now, but in a good way. She gives me balance. And a purpose I didn't know I wanted, or could have."

"And you give her balance."

"But it's all a novelty right now, and that's what scares me. You know, it's like when you get a new toy and that's all you want to play with. Then eventually you get tired of it and totally ignore it."

"You think you'd get tired of Megan?" he asked.

"No, not Megan. But of the role of mothering. That's the novelty, and I'm enjoying the challenge and trying hard not to let my mother issues interfere—you know, trying to do the opposite of what my mother would do. You were right about that, Reid.

"I based a life not on what I wanted but on the opposite of what my mother would do. And I'm working hard to stop it. But I'm still at the point where it's a conscious effort."

"That will come naturally in due course, the way your feelings for Megan have come naturally."

"I do love her."

"Then adopt her. Simple as that."

Keera glanced over at the child, who'd managed to smear her strawberry yogurt from ear to ear. It was like she was wearing a pink beard. So cute, so innocent.

"I want to." She swiped at the tears beginning to roll down her cheeks. Great, fat droplets of grief that were ripping through her soul for so many things. "But is love enough?"

"Love's enough, Keera. Trust me, no matter what else happens, love is what gets you through. Loving Megan is enough. It's where it starts, and everything else builds from there. So now it's time to trust yourself. You're not the wounded little girl any more. You're the woman who has the opportunity to care for another wounded little girl. You'll make her life better, the way she'll make your life better. And I'm speaking from experience on that one."

"This isn't easy, Reid," she said, swatting at her tears and sniffling.

"The right decisions seldom are easy." He pulled her

into his arms. "Weeks ago I met this stubborn, opinionated woman who didn't like kids. At least, not in the sense that she wanted to deal with them on a day-to-day basis. Now look at her, raising one, loving one, her heart breaking over one. I don't think it's a tough decision. In fact, I think it may be the easiest decision you'll ever make."

He pulled his cellphone from his pocket and handed it to her. "Make the call. You'll never forgive yourself if you don't."

Taking the phone from his hand, she nodded and swallowed hard. "I still think you'd make the better parent," she said, then dialed Consuela.

"Dr. Adams," Brett Hollingsworth said from the door, "could I speak to you privately in the hall?"

Keera reached out and squeezed his hand as she waited for her call to go through. "Want me to come with you?" she asked.

"I'm fine. And I'll feel better after I know you got through to Consuela."

"Thanks, Reid," she said, as he turned and walked away.

His response was a lackluster nod to accompany his slumped shoulders, and she wished to heaven she could make the walk with him, but she couldn't. She knew that. And her heart hurt so badly for him she could barely talk when Consuela came on the line.

"Well, the good news is it's not her appendix. Nothing in her blood work indicates she's having a recurrence of her leukemia either."

Finally, Reid let go of the breath he'd been holding. "Then what is it?"

"We think it's mesenteric adenitis." An inflammatory

condition that often resulted from general weakening in cancers associated with the lymph system. "Not sure yet, because we're ruling out other things. But the lymphs in her belly are swollen. Combine that with her nausea and vomiting, her lack of appetite, the malaise, fever, and she's been complaining of a headache—all pretty classic symptoms."

"Could she have picked up a virus that caused it?"

"My best guess right now would be yes. Maybe something as simple as stomach flu. It's all interrelated with her leukemia, and not all that uncommon."

"I—I don't know what to say. I mean, that's good news. No, it's great news!"

"What's great news?" Keera said, walking up behind him.

"Mesenteric adenitis."

"Whoa, that's an offbeat kind of diagnosis." She smiled. "But a good one. And it makes sense."

"Well, I still want to do the imaging," Brett continued, "but we've ruled out appendicitis as well as leukemia."

Keera slipped her hand into Reid's. "So do the imaging. STAT," she said happily.

"Already ordered," he said. "Just wanted Dr. Adams to know what we're thinking right now."

"I'm thinking I was too involved to even consider..." Reid shut his eyes, drew in a deep breath. "Whatever consents you'll need, you know you've got them."

"What I want to do is let her sleep the next few hours then see if we can get the imaging in late afternoon, early evening. In the meantime, get her started on fluid and electrolyte replacement, and an anti-inflammatory. Then treat other symptoms as they arise and keep our fingers crossed that we caught this early enough that no other symptoms will come up. Oh, and I do want to watch her overnight in the ICU, but by morning I think she'll be stable enough to transfer to the floor."

"I don't know what to say," Reid said.

"For, what, the third or fourth time today?" Keera teased.

Brett punched him on the shoulder. "Well, I say go get some sleep. You look like hell and in a few hours I think your little girl's going to feel better than you do."

"Thank you," Reid said, as Brett walked away.

"Don't thank me. Thank Keera. She's the one who dragged us all down here in the middle of the night and kept pushing us to find the problem."

"Thank you," he whispered, bending to kiss her on the lips.

"He's right, you know. You do look worse than Emmie does."

"That's what parenthood does to you sometimes."

"Guess I'm about to find out," she said.

"Really? It going to happen?"

"It's going to happen. I'm going to adopt her."

Suddenly Reid pulled her into his arms and the kiss he gave her was neither circumspect nor proper for a hospital corridor, but he didn't care because everything was right in his world. More than right. Everything was perfect.

"Well, Brax has Megan and Emmie down at the stable looking at the new foal, and Deanna and Beau took Allie, along with their kids, Lucas and Emily, to go get ice cream. So we're finally alone. At long last."

"It's a nice place. I can see why you love raising your girls here. I'm hoping Megan and I get some weekend invitations to come down every once in a while."

"See, that's the thing. I wasn't planning on weekend invitations. They're too disruptive."

She saw the twinkle in his eyes, didn't know what it meant. "So we're not invited?"

"That's the other thing. You are, but not in the way you expected."

"What are you trying to say, Reid? I'm not invited, but I am?"

"I was thinking like more in the permanent sense. And before you shoot me down, I know you vowed never to get married again, never have a serious relationship, whatever that nonsense was you kept dropping on me at camp. But that was then, and you're a mom now who needs a dad for her daughter. And I'm a dad who needs a mom for my daughters."

"What about the other part?"

"Which part?"

"Where you're a man who needs a wife for himself? Because the rest are good reasons, but that's the best one. That, and the one where I love you more than I can even tell you. For me it was love at first sight. Or else I would have shoved Megan in your arms and gotten the heck out of there. But when you opened the door..." She shook her head.

"You had me at the door, Doc Adams, and I really didn't want to be had. Although deep down I knew I did, even though I didn't think I could ever be what you needed."

"You were, Keera. I needed to make you see who you really were, though. Who you really are. Really can be. So, can you do this? Because I don't want you making all the compromises while I sit here and do nothing. You're going to get two other children in the deal, and that's a huge compromise, because they want you to be their real mommy."

"I'm not compromising a thing because I want to be their real mommy. I love those girls, Reid. Yours, mine...

ours. But you do have to understand that I'm the one who needs to make the biggest change. For the first time in my life, though, I want to. Because I need to. There's nothing else that will ever make me complete the way you and the girls do. And it scares me how much I'll need your help in this. Maybe every day for the rest of my life. But I want to make the change. Walk away from everything I was and walk towards everything I want to be. As long as you know exactly what you're getting."

"Oh, I know. And, seriously, all your aversions to children, family and marriage scared me for a while, or else I would have proposed maybe the day after I met you. Which was when I think I fell in love with you. Or maybe it was at first sight. I'm still a little foggy on that. The thing is, I saw through you pretty quickly. Saw how much you were trying to hide, or hide behind. And always fighting to prove you were tough, and impervious to the world. Except you weren't, and I knew that."

"Your camp changed me, your girls changed me, Megan changed me. Most of all, you changed me. Made me realize I can have the things I thought I never could. The worst thing anyone could ever know about me is what you know, and it doesn't matter to you."

"Because everything you were in the past turned you into the woman I love today."

"My past isn't over, though. You've got to understand that it may rear its ugly head from time to time. And you may see that stubborn streak come back as well. That's part of who I am."

"Only a small part. And we'll face it together if it does peek in every now and then. No big deal."

"Easy for you to say."

"Easy for me to know, because I know you."

"And I know you."

"But can you be a country GP, give up your surgical practice and settle down to the kind of life we have here? Because we're a very family-centered practice, and our families always come first, no matter what. Which might be a little difficult for you—"

"Not difficult," she interrupted. "Although I still want to keep my surgical practice, just limit it to maybe a couple days a week. An easy flight to Central Valley if the man you're married to is a pilot."

"Married sounds good, doesn't it?"

"Very good. Because for once in my life I think I'll be able to relax, breathe, just enjoy life. And with three daughters to raise, and take shopping!"

"About that shopping, and your choice of clothes for them…"

"What's wrong with my choice of clothes?" she asked.

"Not traditional. Just saying."

"Just saying you think I'm not traditional? Hey, Doc! We've got an hour to kill before anybody misses us. What do you say to going over to your place so I can show you exactly how untraditional the rest of your life is going to be?"

He reached for Keera's hand, then when he had it pulled her roughly into his embrace. "What do you say about going over to *our* place so we can do we do just that?"

* * * * *

Wrap up warm this winter with Sarah Morgan...

Sleigh Bells in the Snow

Kayla Green loves business and hates Christmas.

So when Jackson O'Neil invites her to Snow Crystal Resort to discuss their business proposal... the last thing she's expecting is to stay for Christmas dinner. As the snowflakes continue to fall, will the woman who doesn't believe in the magic of Christmas finally fall under its spell...?

4th October

www.millsandboon.co.uk/sarahmorgan

She's loved and lost — will she ever learn to open her heart again?

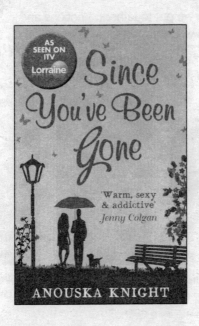

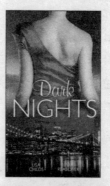
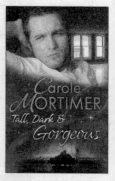

Join the Mills & Boon Book Club

Subscribe to **Medical** today for 3, 6 or 12 months and you could **save over £40!**

We'll also treat you to these fabulous extras:

- 🌹 **FREE L'Occitane gift set worth £10**
- 🌹 **FREE home delivery**
- 🌹 **Rewards scheme, exclusive offers…and much more!**

Subscribe now and save over £40
www.millsandboon.co.uk/subscribeme

The World of Mills & Boon®

There's a Mills & Boon® series that's perfect for you. We publish ten series and, with new titles every month, you never have to wait long for your favourite to come along.

Blaze
Scorching hot, sexy reads
4 new stories every month

By Request
Relive the romance with the best of the best
9 new stories every month

Cherish™
Romance to melt the heart every time
12 new stories every month

Desire
Passionate and dramatic love stories
8 new stories every month